TADUNO'S SONG

TADUNO'S SONG

ODAFE ATOGUN

CANONGATE

Edinburgh · London

Published in Great Britain in 2016 by Canongate Books Ltd,
14 High Street, Edinburgh EH1 1TE

www.canongate.tv

1

British Library Cataloguing-in-Publication Data
A catalogue record for this book is available
on request from the British Library

ISBN 978 1 78211 805 3

Typeset in Goudy Old Style by
Palimpsest Book Production Ltd, Falkirk, Stirlingshire

Printed and bound in Great Britain by Clays Ltd, St Ives plc

For Samuel . . . for the years we could not share

ONE

The morning the letter arrived he was like a man in a shell, deaf to the voices in his head from a distant place, calling him, imploring him with old promises.

It was a dull morning with no hint of sun, no hint of rain, no hint of anything; just a dull morning that brought a letter in a stained brown envelope from his homeland, delivered by an elderly postman wearing horn-rimmed spectacles and boots twice the size of his feet.

Studying the handwriting on the envelope, his eyes lit up in recognition. But then a frown crept across his face and he wondered how a letter simply marked TADUNO – no last name, no address, just Taduno – managed to reach him in a nameless foreign town. He thought of asking the postman how he found him with no address, but because he could not speak the language of the people of that town, he merely gave a small nod of thanks and watched the elderly man drag himself away in his oversized boots until he became a speck in the distance.

The letter changed the tone of his day and he knew, even before he began to read it, that the time had come for him to go back. He had always known that that day would come, but he never suspected it would be prompted by a mysterious letter portending a vague but grave disaster.

He settled into a chair by an open window and studied the empty street. He saw no movement, no life, nothing; just an emptiness that came at him in waves. A small sigh escaped him, and as the barking of a lone dog cracked the quiet neighbourhood, he adjusted his seat for a better view of the street. He saw the dog a little way off, scrawny and lonely, wandering with an invisible burden on its tired back. It was the first and only time he would see a dog in that town, and he suspected that, like himself, it must have strayed into exile from a country governed by a ruthless dictator. He felt sorry for the dog. He shook his head and began to read the letter.

20th February, 19—

Dear Taduno,

I hope you are very well and that the country where you have found refuge is treating you kindly. I know you'll wonder how I managed to get this letter across to you without an address. Well, all I can say is 'where there is a will there is always a way'.

At first I did not want to write because I thought you deserve the opportunity to start life afresh and build new memories. But I must confess that ever since you left, life has been an unbearable torture for me. I have never stopped thinking about you, and I never will. Do you remember all the dreams we shared but never lived, the future we never realised? I remember. I have remembered every day since you left. But that's not why I write this letter.

Forgive me if my letter disrupts the peace you must be enjoying now. Forgive me if it brings back all the bad memories you fled. Forgive me for this invasion of your new life. But I thought I would not be doing you any good by failing to inform you now of what may turn out to be a tragic discovery for you later.

In time to come, should you yield to the pull of your roots, you may be returning home to unpleasant surprises. Since you left, very strange things have been happening in Nigeria, and Lagos particularly has changed in a way I cannot describe with words. I must confess, I don't know exactly what is going on – nobody knows; all I can say is that things are changing drastically here, and the city of Lagos is not the same as we used to know it.

This is why I thought I should write, to encourage you to build a life elsewhere knowing that very soon nothing may remain the same here.

For me, I continue to hold on to old memories. They are all that will be left when there is nothing left. I pray earnestly that you find new memories to cherish.

Look after yourself.

Goodbye.

Lela

By the time he finished reading, it was no longer a morning with no hint of anything. The letter had changed that, and now he felt the urgent need to get some fresh air. He left the letter on the coffee table and went out into the garden where he wandered without any sense of time, troubled by the terribleness of a message he did not understand. He went through the letter again in his mind, very slowly, and he shuddered at the prospect of building a life elsewhere without Lela. Why would she even think like that? What's going on back home? Questions ran across his mind; a familiar fear tugged at him.

*

Hours on, the grumblings of his stomach led him back into the house. In the kitchen, he could not make up his mind what to eat. The indecision killed his hunger, replacing it with a need to read the letter all over again.

The echoes of his footsteps followed him into the living room, but he could not find the letter on the coffee table where he had left it. He looked under the table, all over the floor, everywhere. He searched frantically without luck. And then it occurred to him that, possibly, the elderly postman had returned to get the letter while he was out in the garden. But how could he? Surely he couldn't have gained entrance into the house.

For some reason, he remembered the lone dog. He felt its hopelessness, its loneliness, and he wondered how it was faring in the street.

He searched for the letter all morning, but he couldn't find it; and, telling himself that he did not need to find it to take the decision to return to his homeland, he began earnest preparations to leave a town where he had been living in exile for almost three months.

*

He had arrived in that town with a single bag and the dream of returning home one day to continue the fight to liberate his country from a ruthless dictator.

It was a very beautiful town indeed, and for hours he roamed the largely deserted streets shrouded in secret and ageless silence. The town boasted very stately houses, many unoccupied, as stated by small silver signs posted on low gates. He discovered that every empty house had a key in the front lock, as if waiting to be occupied, begging to be occupied. He wondered at the sheer magnificence of the houses. He wondered at the manicured gardens. He roamed the streets until his legs got weary. And then he settled into a small white house with a big garden in a remote neighbourhood where life is as quiet at midday as at midnight.

He did not make friends, partly because he did not understand the language and partly because he lived on a virtually deserted street. He wondered why there were so many empty houses in the town, why he rarely saw people in the streets. At first he was consumed by fear, knowing he was an illegal occupant of the white house. But as the days went by and no one came to evict him, his fear waned and he settled into the monotony of a safe life far away from the reach of the Nigerian dictator.

The town was a perfect haven for him. No one knew

him and no one made any attempt to know him. He spoke to no one, no one spoke to him. The few people he encountered on his lonely trips to the grocery shop in the centre of town simply stared at him, without hostility, without friendliness, knowing he was a harmless stranger amongst them. The owner of the grocery shop would merely give him a toothless grin as he paid for his groceries. Somehow, he never had any problem knowing the right amount of money to pay. He would carry his grocery bags, one in each hand, and walk quietly back to the white house.

He spent endless hours missing his homeland. He missed Lela so dearly. He missed his guitars too, and he wished he could make beautiful music to lift the quiet spirit of that town. He would sit in the garden of the white house, alone with his thoughts, while silence echoed around him. When he wasn't sleeping, he lived his life in the garden. He ate in the garden, read in the garden and dreamt about his homeland in the garden. And on receiving Lela's letter, it was in the garden that he took the final decision to return home.

He had very little to pack over the following days, and he did so with the slowness of a man whose heart was filled with memories of pain. He thought of going to say goodbye to the owner of the grocery shop, to share his toothless grin one last time. He longed to say some sort of goodbye; a thank-you maybe, for the hospitality he had enjoyed in that town. But knowing how sad goodbyes could be, he told himself it was best to leave with no goodbyes. So he focused on packing his single bag the same way he had arrived with it.

His preparations complete, he paused to reflect on his experience of exile, and he realised that it was far different from anything he had ever heard or read. In exile you live life counting the seconds and minutes and hours, allowing yourself to be consumed by ennui, as indistinct days roll one into another.

*

The day before his departure, he roamed the streets in search of the scrawny dog, eager to know that it was doing well. Everywhere he went he felt eyes peering at him from curtained windows, but he wasn't concerned because he knew that he would be gone in the morning. So he explored the town, as far and fast as his legs would carry him.

He saw faces he had never seen before and discovered places he never knew existed. His search led him on, hour after hour, through near-empty streets and along desolate paths. He searched everywhere, but he failed to find the dog. For a while he was sad; but knowing that the people of that town were very accommodating, he told himself that the dog would find a good home. Comforted by this thought, he returned home to Lagos.

TWO

He arrived not knowing what to expect. While riding home in a taxi from the train station, it came as a surprise to him that the city where he had spent most of his adult life had changed drastically in three months. The smells and noises were still the same, and the people still spoke in so many tongues and tones. Yet there was something which had changed about the city. He could not tell what it was, but with his heart beating unevenly, he began to realise what Lela meant in her letter.

He thought it very strange that no one had recognised him since his arrival. The taxi driver averted his eyes and avoided conversation. He wondered why. For a moment he remembered the legend of a great painter who was forgotten by his own people. Saddened by his fate, the painter had gone to a crowded square where he had drawn a life-size portrait of himself.

Taduno gazed out of the window as the taxi crawled

and then sped through the city. He wondered how someone could find themselves in their own painting.

He arrived home under the cover of darkness and sneaked unnoticed through the back door into the old detached house where he had lived for nearly ten years. He took a deep breath to reacquaint himself with the home which life in exile had denied him. He chose not to turn on the lights so as not to draw the attention of his neighbours. Instead, he lit a candle.

The amount of dust that covered everything amazed him, and he knew that it would take several days to do a thorough cleaning. That could wait. He had more urgent matters to deal with, top of which was getting in touch with Lela to find out exactly what was going on. She lived just three streets away with her parents, and he suspected that she would already be in bed at that time of night. Knowing that she maintained a strict routine of waking up at 5 a.m. to clean her parents' compound before getting ready for work, he made up his mind to catch her first thing in the morning.

He left the candle on his bedside table and fell asleep long before the light burned out.

*

He slept soundly at first, then fitfully. When he awoke, he sensed strongly once again that something had changed about the city.

It was getting on to 4.30 a.m. He spent a few minutes

in the bathroom and was soon ready to leave the house. He opened the front door to the breeze of a cold morning, and turned up his collar for protection. For a moment he took in the empty street, and his heart began to race at the prospect of seeing Lela again after so many months.

He was locking the door behind him when a voice barked at him from the street. 'Who are you?'

It was still dark; he could not make out the face of the person questioning him but recognised the voice as that of Aroli, his neighbour of many years. Aroli was a poet and estate agent, famous in the neighbourhood not for his writing or his job, but for his habit of knocking loudly on people's doors and softening their reaction with a smile. He often told anyone who cared to listen, 'I'm a poet by profession, and an estate agent only by virtue of the fact that poetry cannot put food on my table, in the interim.'

Taduno approached the shadowy figure and was soon able to make out Aroli's face. 'Aroli, it's me,' he whispered. 'I returned last night.'

'You who?'

'Me, Taduno,' he said, raising his whisper and cupping his mouth with his hand.

The two men inched closer until they were peering into each other's face. And then Aroli backed off. 'I don't know you! Who are you?' His voice was a fearful snarl.

Taduno sighed with frustration, certain Aroli was merely trying to pull a prank. 'Come on, Aroli, it's me, Taduno.'

'I don't know you! How did you know my name?' Aroli continued to retreat, putting up his hands in readiness to defend himself.

'Please stop this joke,' Taduno begged. 'I don't want to announce my arrival yet.'

And then Aroli raised an alarm that brought out the entire street. They came out with sleep still in their eyes, carrying sticks and stones. Aroli was not a man of violence, so he planted himself between Taduno and the invading crowd, his hands flailing above his head. He did not want to be responsible for the spilling of a man's blood.

'He says he knows me,' Aroli spoke at the top of his voice. 'Please let's give him a chance to identify himself before we take the law into our hands. Poetic justice may not be necessary after all. Please let's give him a chance to speak.'

There were a few sniggers in the crowd, and everyone seemed to calm down. Aroli had a way of settling people with the funny use of words – usually out of context (poetic licence, he called it) – and with his gentle smile.

Morning light was breaking rapidly through the clouds now, and Taduno could make out the faces of his neighbours. He knew them all, and he called out their names one after the other, in a rush, desperate to save himself from being lynched like a thief. He told them things about themselves. They were all amazed as he spoke, and gradually the sticks and stones fell from their hands. But confusion remained on all their faces, as on his. And as the light of the new day got brighter, it became very clear that, indeed, none of them knew him even though he knew them all.

He told them about his girlfriend Lela, whose letter had prompted him to return home from exile. Yes, they knew

Lela, the pretty light-skinned maths teacher. But, they informed him, 'government agents arrested her two weeks ago', so she was not available to corroborate his claims.

'I received a letter from her a week ago.' His voice was filled with hysteria.

They responded with blank stares.

He looked as confused as they were. And then, realising that the something that had changed about the city was actually something that had changed about him, he began to cry wretchedly.

*

They told him he could stay in the house he claimed to have lived in for ten years, so long as he did not make trouble with anyone. After all, the house had been empty since the owner died many months before. Rather than allow it to turn into a ghost haunt, they figured it was better to let someone stay there.

They saw him as a nice and decent person. According to one elderly man, 'the mystery that unites us will solve itself in due time'. So they let him stay.

Behind his back they whispered that he was a nice man who had obviously lost his mind – a sick man who deserved their compassion.

A dash to Lela's house confirmed his worst fears. He was not who he claimed to be, and Lela had indeed been arrested by government agents.

Lela's seven-year-old brother Judah, who he fondly called Lion of Judah, and with whom he sometimes played street football, gave him the distant look of a stranger. He felt pained to the bone.

'Lion of Judah, it's me, Taduno. We used to play ball together. Last Christmas I bought you the trainers with red lights. You wear them when we play ball.'

Judah studied his face with a frown. Then he shook his head slowly as if to say he could not identify it as that of the uncle who bought him the trainers he loved so much.

Much as Taduno tried to jolt the boy's memory, his eyes failed to light with recognition.

Everywhere he went it was the same story. Friends he had known since childhood claimed they didn't know him. He went round to the houses of relatives scattered across the city. Nobody knew him, but they did all agree on one thing – he was a nice man who had lost his mind. And they smiled at him with pity. As a last resort, he thought of going to the studio where he began his music career, but afraid that the story would be the same, and certain that that would sever his last hold on reality, he decided against it.

He roamed the city like a man knocked senseless by a vicious blow. Not knowing what to do or who to turn to, he returned to his house, which they said belonged to a dead man. First he checked the safe where he had kept his title deed for many years, but he could not find the documents. 'Who am I?' he muttered to himself and began to wander numbly through the house in search of clues.

His spirit lifted when he remembered his photo albums. It occurred to him that they could be the key to resolving his identity. In the albums were a number of photos he had taken with some of his neighbours – at birthday parties, naming ceremonies and other special occasions; photos of him and Lela, some taken on romantic outings, many more in that house of a dead man. He was ecstatic with delight.

For hours he searched desperately for the albums. He searched until sweat was running down his entire body, into his shoes, and every living part of him began to ache. Still, he searched; way past midnight. And as the city slept, gripped in one gigantic nightmare, he finally accepted, with crushing resignation, that his precious albums had been swallowed by the same mystery that erased his identity.

He would not give up. He needed to find something, anything, that connected him to a society that no longer knew him. There had to be something. He remembered the papers; he used to be front-page news before he went into exile. Frantically, he gathered all the old papers in the house and searched through them. But he couldn't find a single mention of himself in any of them. Somehow, he had been erased from the printed pages.

Defeated and exhausted, he joined the city in sleep. When he awoke it was seven o'clock. 'Is it possible that there is some truth in legend?' he asked himself. For several minutes he tossed and turned in bed, and then he drifted into a state of half sleep, and lingered in that state until early evening when the frenetic noises of the city slowly began to ease.

*

Aroli paid him a visit that evening. He knocked on the door in a manner that would have woken the dead.

'Find a seat, please,' Taduno said awkwardly, after letting him in. 'The place is dusty. I haven't had time to clean.'

A huge smile remained plastered on Aroli's face knowing Taduno must still be reeling from his loud knocking.

'I'm sorry about this whole confusion,' Aroli began, 'but I'm sure things will sort themselves out.' He shifted uncertainly in his seat. 'How are you settling in?'

Taduno shrugged and laughed. 'Well, I'm getting used to being a stranger.'

'I'm sure you'll not feel like a stranger for too long. Everybody likes you. They want you to settle in and see yourself as one of us. Let me know if you need anything. Feel free to come round to my place any time. I live three houses away. I . . .'

'I know, Aroli,' he interrupted him. 'I know you live in a two-bedroom apartment in a block three houses away. I know you have a sister called Bukky, who used to live with you; then she got married and moved with her husband to Accra. I know you have a girlfriend called Janet, who you are confused about. I know your name is Rolland, but everyone calls you Aroli. I know you have a fake *Mona Lisa*, which you bought from Ojuelegba, hanging on the wall of your living room, above your thirty-inch Sony TV. I've visited your apartment many times before and you've visited me countless times. I know you, Aroli, I know you well, the poet/estate agent who goes around banging on people's door with a gentle smile. How can I not know you?' A faint smile warmed his face.

Aroli shifted uncomfortably, lost for what to say.

Without bothering to ask whether Aroli wanted a drink,

he went to fetch two bottles of beer from the kitchen. He opened them and passed a bottle to Aroli, and together they drank in silence.

'I guess you must be hungry,' Aroli said, when they finished drinking. 'Let's go and get something to eat.'

They went to Mama Iyabo's restaurant a few streets away where they ate *amala* and *ewedu* soup, and everyone gave him that polite smile normally reserved for strangers. And he smiled back at them in like manner, not because he saw them as strangers, but because he no longer knew himself.

*

He went out in the morning to get some provisions and the papers. Then he returned and locked himself away from the world for seven days and seven nights, hoping that by the time he re-emerged something would have changed about the city and that that something would have changed the city in a way that people would begin to remember him, and he would find Lela again, and all that had forced him to go into exile would have changed too, and it would be a happy homecoming for him after all.

His neighbours became very worried about him. They gathered outside his house every day for those seven days, wondering if he had done something to himself, debating whether to break down the door.

But Aroli implored them not to take a hurried decision. 'After all,' he told them, 'Taduno is a nice man who would not want anything bad to happen to anyone, least of all himself.' And so his neighbours exercised patience. And on the eighth day he emerged. And apart from the fact that his neighbours were delighted to see him, he realised that nothing had changed about the city. Nothing had changed about him either – except that he had grown a full beard.

THREE

It was while shaving off his beard that Taduno experienced his most lucid state since returning from exile; and it occurred to him that losing his identity was not so bad after all. He realised that he was no longer a man on the run from the law, as was the case before. Considering this advantage, he began to see himself as his neighbours saw him – a man with no past – and he realised that if he must find Lela and unravel the mystery that now surrounded him, he must continue to see himself that way.

During the time he had locked himself away from the world, he had agonised over Lela's plight. He wondered why government agents arrested her, a simple teacher – a maths teacher for that matter – who worked only with equations and never involved herself with suppositions or anti-government activities.

He had always taken care not to reveal much of his life as an activist to her. Even when he had to go into exile he had simply left her a note saying 'Where I go I know not'. Could it be that he compromised her with that simple note?

For a while this question haunted him. And then, making up his mind to find out more about Lela's arrest, he returned to her parents' house, where he found Judah kicking a ball on the street with a couple of kids. The boy was the lone star: he had on the trainers with red lights, the others played barefoot.

'Judah,' he called out.

The boy pulled out of the game and walked up to him. He had a smile on his cherubic face, unlike the last time when he wore a confused frown.

Taduno wasn't surprised. Everyone was being so nice to him, Judah no exception. He smiled back at the boy.

'Sorry to interrupt your game.'

'It's okay.' Judah looked down at his trainers and then up at Taduno's face, and it was clear that he still could not connect the two.

'I want to talk to you about your sister.'

The boy nodded eagerly. 'Have you found her?'

'No, I have not, but I'm going to find her.'

Judah beamed. 'Thank you!'

'When was the last time you saw her?'

'The day some men pushed her into the back of a black car, a big black car. It happened right there,' he said, pointing to a spot on the street. 'I was playing football with my friends that evening. I'm always playing football on the street, so I saw it all, I saw the men.'

'How many were they?' Taduno asked, with a faint smile.

'There were four in all. *Anti* Lela was screaming for help, but nobody went to help her, everybody was afraid.'

'What kind of clothes were the men wearing?'

'I don't know. Normal clothes, I think. They had guns and they waved their badges.'

'Did they say where they were taking her?'

'No, they didn't say. They didn't talk to anyone, they just waved their badges. Then they got into their car and drove off leaving so much dust in the air.'

'Did your parents witness the incident?'

'No, they were inside the house. By the time they came running out, the men were gone and only the dust remained.'

He realised that it was pointless questioning Lela's parents as their story would likely be similar to Judah's.

He nodded in thanks and slapped Judah playfully on the back. 'I'll find your sister,' he said, looking into the boy's eyes. 'You can go back to your game.'

'Promise?' the boy said, in an eager voice.

'Yes, I promise.'

They shook hands, and in that moment they both felt something – like the rekindling of an old friendship.

*

He spent the rest of the day deliberating on how to begin his search for Lela. He struck off one idea after the other, until he came to the conclusion that the best place to start was a police station.

At first, the prospect of visiting a police station terrified him; but, encouraged by the knowledge that he no longer had an identity, he took a taxi to the nearest station where he found the sergeant on duty dozing at his desk with a half-eaten cob of corn in one hand.

The tiny office reeked of a terrible odour – a mixture of decayed food, saliva, sweat, urine, morbid fear and stale cigarettes. In spite of the fact that he had been in several police stations before, Taduno felt himself choking.

He rapped a gentle knuckle on the counter.

The Sergeant jumped in his seat and the cob of corn in his hand fell to the floor, disappearing under his desk. Quickly, he picked up his worn beret from his battered desk and slapped it on his head to dignify himself with an air of authority. Then he smiled – a friendly sheepish smile that revealed uneven brown teeth.

'Good afternoon, Sergeant Bello,' Taduno greeted, reading the name tag on the Sergeant's chest.

'Afternoon,' the Sergeant replied. 'How may I help you? In what way may I help you? And what help do you need?'

Taduno was not surprised at the rambling manner of the Sergeant's questions. He was familiar with the ways of policemen, and he knew you must also respond to them in a roundabout way to get results. Or else, they will turn you round and around until they get you so confused you end up confessing to a crime you never committed. And then they will lock you up with a satisfied grin. And when you bribe them, they become your friend. But they tell you that you are still a criminal all the same, and that they are friends of criminals. And they remind you, in their own parlance, 'Police is your friend.'

Taduno laughed to himself. 'Oh yes, you may help me. But before you help me, I think you should know that I want to help you too. And in the end you'll be helping me to help you.'

The Sergeant looked quite impressed by the response of the well-dressed man standing before him – no doubt, a respectable gentleman wise in the ways of the police. He nodded vigorously, a look of satisfaction on his round oily face.

'I agree with you. How may we proceed?'

The smile remained on Taduno's face. 'Before we proceed you may want to pick up your corn. I think it must be somewhere under your desk.'

'True!' The Sergeant bent down and retrieved his corn. He blew on it, then he kept it away on the far end of his desk, to be dealt with later. He turned his attention back to Taduno. 'Yes, we may proceed.' He had a business-like air about him now.

Leaning against the counter, Taduno cleared his throat quietly. 'As I was saying, I need you to help me help you. And after you have helped me I will help you.'

'That makes a lot of sense to me,' the Sergeant beamed, rubbing his hands together. 'Please continue.'

Taduno hesitated for a moment then cleared his throat again. 'I'd like to know what happened to a certain Miss Lela Olaro. She was arrested a couple of weeks ago by government agents.'

Sergeant Bello scratched his head and pretended to

think for several moments. Then he nodded his head slowly, as if it was all coming back to him in a trickle.

'You remember?' Taduno asked eagerly.

'Hmm,' the Sergeant grunted. 'Actually, I'm trying to remember. It is not so easy to remember, you know.'

'Yes, yes, I know. That's why I need you to help me help you. After you have helped me I will help you. Can you tell me what happened to her, please?'

Sergeant Bello scratched his head some more. 'Was she arrested or kidnapped?' he demanded gruffly.

The question caught Taduno by surprise. He thought very quickly, then he asked: 'You tell me, was she arrested or kidnapped?'

Sergeant Bello hesitated.

Taduno pressed. 'I'm only asking so that you'll help me to help you, nothing more.' He turned on a foolish smile.

'True, true, I understand, my brother. I need plenty of help actually. Things are very difficult at home.'

'So?'

'She was kidnapped by the government,' the Sergeant said in a whisper, looking furtively around to make sure none of his colleagues was approaching. 'They only tried to make it look like an arrest.'

Taduno did not show his surprise. 'I would think that government agents arrest people, not kidnap them?'

'You'd be surprised,' the Sergeant chuckled.

'Where was she taken? Why was she kidnapped?'

The Sergeant's face hardened. 'I've helped you enough to help me!' he hissed.

Taduno slipped a 500-naira note across the counter and left the station quietly.

*

Rather than take a taxi, he decided to walk home. He covered the six-kilometre distance in two hours without paying any attention to the bustling city life that raced past him. He arrived home tired and consumed by fear for the woman he loved.

Aroli was sitting on his doorstep waiting for him, glancing through an old paper in a distracted manner. He rose to his feet when he saw Taduno approaching.

None of his other neighbours paid him any attention. They busied themselves with their evening chores, their curiosity about him having died since he re-emerged into the world. As far as they were concerned, he was now one of them, having shown that he could survive seven whole days without seeing sunlight and without running mad or hurting himself.

'I haven't seen you around all day,' Aroli said, after they had exchanged greetings.

'I went out to attend to an urgent matter.'

'I see.' Aroli sounded curious.

Taduno fiddled in his pocket for his keys and opened the door. 'Please come in.' Somehow he managed not to show just how troubled he was.

'Wow!' Aroli exclaimed the moment he stepped into the house. 'Looks like you've been doing a lot of cleaning. The place is spotless!'

'It took me seven days to achieve,' Taduno said.

'Was that why you locked yourself away?'

'Not really. Yes, I did a lot of cleaning, but it was more a time of soul-searching for me.'

'I see.'

'Take a seat, please.'

They sat opposite each other.

'You said you went out to attend to an urgent matter?'

'Yes, I have been trying to follow Lela's trail.'

Aroli sat up. 'What have you discovered?'

Taduno hesitated.

'You can trust me,' Aroli assured him.

'Lela was not arrested. She was kidnapped.'

'Kidnapped by who?' Aroli asked, a frown on his face.

'By the government.'

Aroli's jaw dropped. 'Where did you get that information?'

'From a certain sergeant in a certain police station,' he replied, not keen to reveal his source.

'I don't understand. Why would the government kidnap Lela?' Aroli scratched his head.

'I asked myself the same question, and the answer is not so pleasant.'

'Which is?'

'Security agents arrest you if you are believed to have committed an offence. But if the government sees you as a threat, they kidnap you.'

Aroli scratched his head some more, slowly, his brain ticking loudly. 'That means Lela must be in grave danger.'

'You get the picture.'

They fell into silence.

'What are you going to do?' Aroli asked, at last.

'I intend to find her.' Taduno's voice was grim with determination.

Aroli shut his eyes tightly, as if trying to erase a bad memory, perhaps a reality too difficult to accept. 'I don't know how to put this,' he began, uncertainly.

'Put what?' Taduno raised his brows in question.

'You showed up claiming to be somebody we know. We all see you as a man who has lost his identity – in fact, a man who has lost his mind. But I have been worried since that first morning, and my mind tells me something is not quite right.'

Taduno remained silent.

Aroli continued. 'You know too much about us to be a stranger, too much to be a man who has lost his mind.'

'What are you driving at?'

'I'm worried that it could be the rest of us who have lost our minds. I'm worried that a man who has lost his mind cannot be as sane as you are. You know so much about us, yet we know nothing about you. Is it possible that we are the ones who have forgotten the past? Honestly, I suspect that this could be the case.

'Tell me about your life. I mean the life you used to live before we forgot you. I need to know about you. I need to know so that I can remember all that I have forgotten.' Aroli was beginning to sound desperate.

Taduno sighed, touched by Aroli's candour. 'At first the life I lived was simple. But then things changed and it became complex.' He shook his head. 'It's not something I can talk about now.'

Aroli nodded his understanding. He rose to leave. The look of confusion on his face deepened; a look that wanted answers to so many questions. In a quiet voice he said, 'I'm prepared to help you find Lela, if you need my help.'

Taduno reasoned that it would do him no harm to take Aroli into his confidence. 'I intend to go to the police station again tomorrow,' he said. 'You can come with me if you are not busy.'

Aroli agreed to go with him.

FOUR

The following morning they took a yellow taxi to the police station. The taxi had been recently repainted, and it wasn't until they got into the back seat that they realised that the taxi was repainted to attract passengers. It looked very clean on the outside, but on the inside it was battered and smelled of damp.

It was too late for them to climb out by the time they discovered the ruse, so they made themselves as comfortable as possible on the torn leather seat which Taduno suspected was lice-infested. And as the taxi drove them to the police station, he filled Aroli in about his encounter the previous day with Sergeant Bello.

'He could be the key to finding Lela,' he concluded. 'He knows something, but I doubt if he would want to share what he knows with us at the police station. He was not comfortable talking to me yesterday.'

'What do you suggest?'

'I suggest we meet him on neutral ground.'

'Makes sense to me,' Aroli agreed.

'But we must be careful the way we approach him. Policemen can be very difficult people.'

'I get you.'

They made the rest of the journey in silence.

Luck was on their side. They found Sergeant Bello alone in the office, dozing; a man with nothing meaningful to do, with no time for anything meaningful. The sound of approaching footsteps woke him out of his reverie, and he put on a smile and his worn beret, which he hurriedly picked up from his battered desk.

'Good afternoon, Sarge,' Taduno greeted. 'Remember me?'

'Ah, good afternoon! Of course, I remember you! How can I forget my friend?' The Sergeant smiled expansively.

Taduno smiled back. 'Friends are meant to remember friends, not forget them. I'm glad you remember me!'

For a moment the Sergeant's face hardened. 'Who's this?' he asked, pointing at Aroli.

'Oh, this is my very good friend, Aroli. Together we want to help you to help us. You know it's better for two to help one than for one to help one.' Taduno laughed merrily to dispel the Sergeant's fear.

'I see what you mean!' The Sergeant laughed too.

Aroli joined in the laughter. And together they all laughed merrily, like three idiots.

'So?' Sergeant Bello asked, when their laughter had died down.

'Yeah, we're thinking . . . we're thinking you should have dinner with us tonight somewhere nice.'

'Oh no, no, no!' Sergeant Bello shook his head. 'Dinner sounds okay to me, but not anywhere nice. I'm not used to nice. Nice is a mere waste of money.'

'In that case we could go somewhere not so nice and not so bad.' Taduno demonstrated with his hands, that smile of an idiot still on his face. 'How about that?'

Sergeant Bello nodded with satisfaction. 'That sounds better. I'll be off duty by six. Just remember, nowhere nice. I don't like nice. I don't like nice at all!'

The three of them laughed loudly. And as Taduno and Aroli made to leave, Sergeant Bello stretched out his hand. 'You are forgetting something,' he said, in a frosty voice.

Taduno slipped a 500-naira note into his hand.

The Sergeant kept his hand outstretched. '"It's better for two to help one." Those were your words.'

Taduno shrugged and added another 500-naira note.

*

Their rendezvous was an open-air restaurant situated along a canal that carried half the city's dirt. The restaurant was poorly lit, and it was certainly not nice, but not so bad by Sergeant Bello's standard.

Their orders arrived promptly, and they ate quietly – Taduno and Aroli with relaxed looks on their faces; Sergeant Bello with a sombre look on his.

Under the poor light, Taduno had the opportunity to study Sergeant Bello away from the police station. And he was surprised to see the face of the city – a city battered by a regime that used hopeless people like Bello to perpetuate itself.

They finished eating and moved to an open-air bar, still along the canal, where people were drinking and murmuring, drinking and murmuring against the government, and their anger kept rising with their drunkenness. And their voices became so loud nothing they said made sense any more. And all that filled the air in that garden of drinking people was bitter anger against the government. And Sergeant Bello could take it no more – knowing he was against the people, and on the side of evil. And he felt sad knowing that the same people he was against murmur not for their own good, but for his as well.

Taduno sensed Sergeant Bello's state of mind. He cleared his throat. 'When the people murmur like this, it means there is hope for the future,' he said, trying to sound cheerful.

'Maybe. But what hope is there for someone like me?' Sergeant Bello was forlorn. He drank some beer.

'The same hope there is for us all,' Aroli explained. 'The same hope we share as a society.'

Sergeant Bello gave a small bitter laugh. 'How can I share the same hope with these people when I'm a part of what they murmur against?'

'Regardless of which side we are on, hope is universal. When you begin to hope, you begin to murmur against that which hinders you. And when you murmur, change is bound to come.' Aroli shook his head. 'I wish I could explain it better.'

'You've explained it well enough.' There was a distant

31

look on Sergeant Bello's face. 'I have enough education to understand your words. And you know what?'

'What?' Taduno and Aroli asked as one.

'I'm beginning to think there's hope for me after all.' A weak smile spread across the Sergeant's face.

Taduno and Aroli exchanged looks.

'Why did you suggest dinner?' Sergeant Bello asked.

Taduno went to the point. 'I need more information about Lela. Why was she kidnapped?'

Sergeant Bello looked thoughtful.

'Why was she kidnapped?' Taduno persisted.

'Government is looking for her boyfriend. He is a musician who used his music to cause trouble for government. They can't find her boyfriend, so they kidnapped her – as a ransom.'

'So it's her boyfriend the government is really after?'

'Yes. If they find him and get him to sing favourably about government, she will be released. Otherwise, she will be killed. They are afraid that his music could start a revolution and topple the government.'

'But she is innocent.'

Sergeant Bello laughed quietly.

'Government does not believe in innocence.'

They drank in silence for a while. And then Taduno asked: 'What's the name of the man the government is looking for?'

'They don't know his name, and the girl would not tell. They only know him as a great musician with a magnetic voice.'

'Have they got a picture of this man?'

'No, they don't. They used to know his name; they used

32

to have his picture. But then something happened, something strange nobody can remember, and he became a man with no name and no face. They think he is at the heart of a sinister conspiracy to topple the government.'

'So the government is looking for a man they don't know, a man with no name and no face?' Taduno wore a bewildered look.

'Yes, but the girl Lela knows, and they are trying to make her reveal his identity.'

'And the boyfriend must become a praise-singer for the government if they are to release her?'

'Yes.'

'Where are they holding her?'

'CID headquarters. But I don't advise you to go there! You'll only get yourselves arrested and tortured.'

'By the way,' Aroli spoke slowly, 'how would the government identify the man they are looking for if he has no name and no face?'

'By his voice,' Sergeant Bello replied. 'His voice is his identity. He has the most wonderful voice in the world. No other human being sings like him . . .'

A slight pause.

'Look, by telling you all these things, I'm simply joining my voice to those of the people, hoping that my little contribution will make a difference.' The Sergeant shifted uncomfortably in his seat. 'As I said before, government does not believe in innocence. If they ever get to know all that I have told you, my life would be worth nothing. So as far as I'm concerned, I never met you two and I don't know you as friends of Lela's.'

They finished their beer. Taduno settled the bill. And they stood up to go. To both Taduno and Aroli's surprise, Sergeant Bello refused to take money in exchange for the information he had given them. 'Take it as my contribution to the murmurings of the people,' he said.

*

It was easy for Taduno to tell Aroli his story after that.

'I used to live a simple life at first. I used to be a musician and all I sang was love songs – songs that encouraged people to live as one, to love without asking for love in return, to give without thinking of receiving,' he explained, pacing the small living room of Aroli's apartment.

It was his first time in the apartment since returning from exile, and everything was just the way he used to know it. The fake *Mona Lisa* still hung on the wall above the Sony television. The sofas were still the same, the ceiling fan still had the same hum, and the walls of the living room were still as bright as ever – a bright yellow that always reminded him of a nursery.

He continued.

'And then everything changed, and I began to sing against injustice and oppression. Everything changed when the June 12th presidential election was annulled and the legitimate winner was thrown in jail. Through my music I became a force, a fierce enemy of the government.'

'But your name's not on the wanted list published by the government some time ago,' Aroli interrupted.

'That's because you all forgot me – my family, friends,

neighbours, the government – the entire country forgot me.'

A short silence.

'So you started using your music to attack government,' Aroli prodded, eager for him to continue his story.

Taduno stopped pacing and dropped into a chair.

'Yes, I became an activist, a thorn in the flesh of government. The President's soldiers beat me up on many occasions, sometimes leaving me for dead. They burned my car and closed my bank accounts. I remained unyielding. On many occasions the President tried to persuade me to give up, promising to make me very rich. But I turned him down, and I continued to fight him with my music. And then his soldiers threatened to kill me.'

'So you went into exile?'

'No, I continued to be a very vocal critic of the regime through my songs. Then they murdered the winner of the June 12th election in detention. The whole country erupted; the regime used the army and the police to subdue the protests. I realised that it was possible to depose the regime with music, so I continued to fight them with my songs.

'And then they banned all record shops from selling my music. The army invaded the shops and confiscated all my records. They invaded my house, any house where my records could be found, and they seized every copy of my records. And they burned them all so that not a single copy of any of my records can be found anywhere today. I guess that was when every record of me was erased from all your memories. I no longer existed because there was no way I could continue to exist without my music. My music was me, and they took it away from me. That was when I gave up the struggle and went into exile.' A deep sigh escaped him.

'Yes, I know it now. The government took my identity away from me and destroyed it. They mutilated me and turned everyone against me – my family, my friends, my neighbours, the entire country. They ground me into the dust. And now even they can no longer recognise me because they destroyed every bit of me.'

'What happened to your band members?'

'I didn't need a band for my kind of music. My music compares to storytelling – it is best sung by one person. Two people cannot weave an enchanting story. I told stories with my music and the only musical instrument I used was the guitar. I had over thirty guitars. The President's soldiers destroyed them all. I was to discover later that the many beatings I received affected my vocal cords. My voice has never been the same.'

'So you are actually the man the government is looking for, Lela's boyfriend,' Aroli spoke, thoughtfully.

'Yes, and I must convince the government that I'm their man if they are to release her. Sadly, nobody remembers me and I no longer have the voice to prove I am the musician they are looking for.'

He dropped his head in dismay, remaining like that for several minutes. And then he looked up with a glimmer of hope in his eyes. 'I think I should just turn myself in and tell them I'm Lela's boyfriend.'

'No,' Aroli said, shaking his head. 'As you have said,

nobody remembers you. Without your voice government will only see you as an imposter, and that could get you into serious trouble.'

Taduno saw Aroli's point and nodded.

They talked a bit more without agreeing on what to do. The street was asleep when he left Aroli's place. He went straight to bed. For a long time he lay fidgeting in the darkness, thinking of Lela and of himself, and he wondered what would happen to both of them if, in the end, nobody remembered him.

FIVE

He came alive with hope in the morning when he found a letter from Lela in his mailbox. It came in a stained brown envelope similar to the one he had received in exile, and it bore only his first name, no last name, no address. In the living room, his hands trembling slightly, he sat down to read the letter.

14th March, 19—

Dear Taduno,

I hope this letter finds you well. I had to write, to tell you that I have been arrested by the President's soldiers.

I don't understand exactly why I'm being held, but I think it is connected to the fact that the government is after you. They say I'm an accomplice – to what? – I do not know. They have interrogated me countless times, asking me to tell them where to find you but I cannot tell what I do not know. They asked me all manner of stupid questions: they want to know what you look like,

38

where you live. They don't even remember your name;
they only refer to you as my boyfriend. I don't understand
what is going on.

I'm well. I have learned to be a woman of faith and
courage. I remember you once told me that holding on
to our faith till the end is what matters, even if we fail
to realise our miracle. So I will not allow them to break
me.

I hope they will release me if they can't find you. If
you receive this letter, keep it a secret. I don't know what
they will do to you if you fall into their hands.

I will try to write to you again soon. Please keep me
in your prayers. I miss you so much.

Love you always,
Lela

Taduno's eyes were moist with tears by the time he finished reading. He read the letter again, hoping that it would throw up a clue, but he felt only pain and frustration. Finally, not knowing what to do, he got a pen and paper and began to write to Lela. He did not put a date or address on the letter; he wanted his words to reach her without the barrier of time and place.

He finished writing. He wept as he folded the letter into a brown envelope. Somehow, he thought, brown envelopes are best for delivering secrets. As tears rolled down his face onto the envelope, he realised why the envelopes in which Lela sent her letters had stains: the stains were teardrops, the pain she felt, carried across time and place. Now, as he watched his tears drying up on the envelope, he felt hope, knowing that she would be reminded of his feelings for her upon receiving the letter.

Not until he had sealed the envelope did it occur to him that he had no clue where to send the letter. For a while he was lost in thought, but seeing no way of getting the letter to Lela, he went outside and left it in his mailbox. And, hoping that whoever delivered her letter to him would find it and take it to her, he took the padlock off the box.

*

He hid the letter he received from Lela where no one could find it. For her sake, he reminded himself, he must not allow anyone, not even Aroli, to know about it. Her words kept echoing in his mind: 'If you receive this letter, keep it a secret.' Although he felt very sad, he also felt relief knowing that she was alive. And now all he had to do to secure her release was learn to sing again. He became filled with a sense of urgency and hope. He realised that if he learned to sing again he could stir the world's memory with his voice and they would remember all that they had forgotten about him. And then he would praise the President with his music and secure the release of the woman he loved!

'I have to learn to sing again,' he said, when Aroli visited him that morning. He was upbeat, but his eyes were tired.

'I think we should secure Lela's release before you turn your attention to reviving your career,' Aroli said, studying his face. 'Get some sleep. You look tired.'

He ignored Aroli's concern. 'Look, my voice is as good as a croak at the moment. There's no way I can convince the regime I'm their man with that kind of voice. I must learn to sing again to secure Lela's release. Don't you see?'

Aroli gave a slow nod of understanding.

Taduno continued. 'If I learn to sing again I will be able to convince the regime I'm their man. And then I can praise the government with my music and get them to release Lela.' He was excited. Although he felt the strong urge to tell Aroli about the letter, he remembered Lela's warning.

'In which case you'll be supporting an evil regime,' Aroli said quietly.

'It's the only way to secure Lela's release.'

Aroli gritted his teeth. He saw no other way.

*

They went out to buy a guitar from a second-hand shop, and then they got something to eat. Returning to Taduno's house, they spent the rest of the day in the upper room where he used to rehearse his songs. For over thirty minutes he strummed the guitar. The music it produced was melodious, dreamy; and it transported Aroli back to a time and place he struggled unsuccessfully to recall.

A smile lingered on Taduno's face as he played his guitar. He played it in very simple tones, eyes closed. Carried away by the moment, he opened his mouth to sing a song from another time, a love song about a beautiful woman. But the sound of his voice caused everything to fall apart. He shook his head, struggling to hold back his tears.

His voice sounded terrible. He flung the guitar aside, and for a long time he simply stared at the wall.

*

'Do you want to try again?' Aroli asked later.

Taduno responded by picking up his guitar, and he began to stroke the strings with feathery fingers. His music poured forth, slowly, patiently. He played for hours, eyes closed, making no attempt to sing this time. Sweat beads stood out on his face like golden dew. His shirt became soaked. His music transported them away from that room to another world. It was a unique experience for Aroli – music without words – yet, he understood the meaning of his song. He knew it was the song of a man broken and rejected by a society very dear to his heart, an adagio of pain, played so beautifully even time became still.

They both opened their eyes when the song came to an end.

'Your music is out of this world,' Aroli complimented.

'Thank you.'

'It was good you did not attempt to sing. If you keep playing with that kind of passion you will discover your voice again.'

Taduno nodded. 'I need the right inspiration,' he said, as if talking to himself.

'How did you use to get inspiration?' Aroli asked.

'From the street, from the suffering on the street, from

seeing so much injustice, from every little act of love shown by one person to another, from the struggles of every day, from the collective joys we share.'

'You must find that inspiration again.'

'Yes,' he agreed. And then he told Aroli about TK, the music producer who gave him his break when he first came to pursue his dream in the city as a teenager. 'He was a very good man, very passionate about music,' he concluded.

'Oh yes, everyone knows TK, the music producer who got on the wrong side of government. One of his artists got him into trouble with the government. And going by all you have told me, you must be that artist. It makes more sense to me now. So it is true that we are the ones who forgot you, the ones who lost our minds . . .'

A short silence followed.

'I'm tempted to pay him a visit,' Taduno spoke his thought aloud, 'but I'm afraid he wouldn't remember me, just like everyone else.'

'It may be worth trying. You never can tell.'

*

Time became so slow that every tick was an agonising reminder of Lela's plight. The letter he had written to her remained in the mailbox and all he could do was focus on practice. Other than playing his guitar – without making any attempt to sing – he had nothing else to do. So he allowed Aroli to drag him to Mama Iyabo's restaurant every now and then for a meal. 'So you don't starve yourself to death,' Aroli would say. And they would eat among people who gave him polite smiles reserved for strangers. And he would listen as Aroli shared jokes with them. And he would wonder about them, how they could be so different when they did not realise that you knew so many secrets about them.

He understood that Aroli was attempting to connect him back to society, to his chief source of inspiration. He did not resist, but he did not encourage him either. He simply enjoyed whatever intimacies his interaction brought. And by so doing, he discovered that he could smile and laugh again, even though the underlying fear in the depth of his soul remained.

On a Friday night, exhausted from playing his guitar, Aroli dragged him to the bar along the slow-rushing canal. The place was so packed the open air was bursting. It was packed with all classes of people – the upper class, the middle class, the lower class, and the classless class.

They were all drinking and murmuring against the government. It was mostly in bars that people found the courage to speak openly. So they poured out their venom. And they drank their beer and ate roasted fish with pepper and onions and soggy chips.

Even though the music was loud in that garden bar, the voices of the people drowned the music. Arguments rose and fell. Everyone wanted to be heard, no one wanted to be quiet. Everyone was gripped by Friday night fever. Taduno was not left out as he drank bottle after bottle of beer. He smiled back at the pretty and not so pretty girls who smiled at him. And he actually took time to gaze at them, and even to wonder about them.

'You haven't mentioned Janet since I returned,' Taduno observed in a rare moment of light-heartedness.

Aroli made a face. 'She left me. Said I was not giving her the stability she needed.'

'Sorry to hear that.' He wished he hadn't brought up the topic.

'It's okay. I mean, I have moved on.' Aroli shrugged.

Aroli's tone of voice piqued Taduno's curiosity.

'Anyone new, any new one?'

Aroli laughed. 'Not really. I'm taking a break.'

'Taking a break?'

'Women are too much hassle.'

Taduno took a long pull at his drink.

Aroli gulped some beer too and wiped his lips with the back of his hand. 'I don't need women now, I need money.' He laughed to himself.

The voices of the revellers began to get louder, much louder than the afro music blaring from four giant speakers which shook with fright at the intensity of the music emanating from them.

At a nearby table an argument broke out between two men: one with a long beard, the other with a bald head, two opposite people. The man with the long beard was tall; the man with the bald head was short. And their argument went in opposite directions.

'Mr President is the Antichrist,' the man with the long beard said loudly.

'How can he be the Antichrist?' the man with the bald head countered. 'He is just an evil dictator.'

'I say he is the Antichrist! Check out his record. He

started out by running the Nigerian army all by himself. Then he overthrew the civilian government and began to rule the country all by himself. Next he will want to rule the whole of West Africa, then Africa, and then he will rule the whole world all by himself. He will unify the world under one government, and then we will all be forced to take the mark of the beast. And you tell me he is not the Antichrist?'

'I disagree. The North Korean dictator is the Antichrist. He will destroy Japan, then America. Then he will force all other countries of the world to bow to him. And he will become the Supreme Leader of the whole world.'

'You don't know what you are saying.'

'Look, let me tell you, all the President wants is to become the richest man in the world, nothing more. He is not interested in becoming the Antichrist and ruling the whole world. Call him a thief, call him a looter of our national treasury, but certainly not the Antichrist.'

The argument went back and forth until it ended in a brawl. As bottles and chairs started flying, Aroli got to his feet. 'I think it's time to leave,' he said.

Taduno grinned. The people were beginning to inspire him again.

*

He played his guitar all night that night, alone in the upper room. He played quietly. His music told the story of two opposite people, one tall and one short; one with

46

a long beard and the other a bald head, two brothers who wanted to kill each other over nothing.

As night got sleepier, he dimmed the lights and hid himself in the shadows drawn across the room. Peace settled upon him. He moved around in a slow dance; and, seeing himself as never before, he realised that he had become one with the shadows in that room.

SIX

His practice sessions got more intense as the days went by. Most times he practised alone while Aroli went about the business of earning a living as an estate agent, taking *okada* rides from one appointment to the next, sweating to sell and buy houses for people, or to find them affordable accommodation, often with very frustrating results.

The rest of Taduno's neighbours began to take an interest in him once again. They wondered why he locked himself away for long hours, sometimes for a whole day. Driven by renewed curiosity about a man who had made a strange entry into their lives, they would gather on the street outside his door, and listen, entranced, to the beautiful music that floated from an open upper window. They wondered why his voice did not accompany the music of his guitar; so they waited, hoping to hear the sound of his voice, curious to know what it sounded like in song.

But all they heard was the faint music of his guitar. And they did not know that the reason why they did not hear him sing was because he was afraid to hear the sound of his own voice.

*

Sometimes, Judah came to watch him play his guitar. Their friendship was growing. The boy would just sit with his hands on his cheeks and wonder at the beauty of his music. He found it amazing that he understood the meaning of his wordless songs, and he could not understand by what magic the strings of his guitar responded to his touch with words so simple and colourful.

'The song you just played is for *Anti* Lela,' the boy told him one day.

'You can tell?' he responded with a smile.

'Of course I can tell. I can tell you miss her so much.'

'Yes, I miss her so much, and I'm doing everything possible to find her.'

'I know you will find her soon,' the boy said hopefully. 'Your music will help you to find her.'

'Yes, I will find her soon,' he replied sadly. 'You see, my voice is bad at the moment. I need to discover it to find Lela.'

The boy nodded in understanding.

And he played yet another song, about a boy and a man, two people who loved a woman so dearly it was difficult to tell who loved her most. He knew that the woman could hear his song from a distant place, and this knowledge lifted him with inspiration as he danced with practised steps in tune with his music.

*

After a week of endless rehearsals, playing the guitar without attempting to sing, he found his way, in the company of Aroli, into the heart of Mushin, to the studio where he started his music career. On the taxi ride to the studio, he was overcome by a flood of memories.

He recalled that morning in June, almost twenty years ago, when he first walked into the studio as an eighteen-year-old. He had learned of the studio days after he arrived in the city on a rickety bus from the village, with a big dream and a battered guitar which his father had given him as a birthday gift. Intrigued by the name 'The Studio of Stars', he made up his mind that it would be the studio that would make him famous.

And so, early one morning, a month or so after arriving in the city, he found his way to the studio. His heart was beating unevenly, and all he could think of was whether they would accept his kind of music. He arrived at the studio and walked into a brightly lit corridor, with his battered guitar dangling from his shoulder, and the first person he encountered was a short squat man with an Afro cut, dressed in a colourful *buba* top and jeans. He thought the man looked funny in his odd combination of native top and western trousers. And his nerves suddenly disappeared as he laughed quietly. He realised that the man was laughing too, quietly. But he did not know why the man was laughing. He did not know that the man was laughing at his battered guitar and cropped trousers, like Michael Jackson's, and his dusty Old Testament sandals.

They faced each other in the brightly lit corridor – the squat middle-aged man and the skinny teenager with a big dream and a battered guitar.

'What brings you here, boy?' The man had a rich voice, and there was an amused look on his face.

Taduno sobered up instantly. 'I came to make music,' he stammered.

'What kind of music do you sing?' Something about the teenager had seized the attention of the man.

'The kind of music that tells stories,' Taduno replied naively.

'All music tells a story,' the man responded.

'Well, my music tells a special kind of story.' Taduno could feel his confidence returning.

'Would you play me your music?' the man asked, in a gentle voice.

Taduno hesitated.

'My name is TK, I own this studio.'

'Oh!' Taduno exclaimed, unable to say anything more.

'I would like to hear your music,' TK continued, with an encouraging smile. He had been in music the whole of his life and something told him the young man standing before him was special. 'Come with me. Please?'

Taduno disregarded TK's invitation. He unslung his guitar from his shoulder, and right there in the corridor, under the brightly lit bulbs, he began to strum the guitar. The battered guitar produced a mesmerising tune. And then he began to sing about two funny men. One laughed because he thought the other was funny. And the other thought the first one was funny and laughed too. And the two of them laughed, not knowing that they were both funny men.

It was a short piece; it screamed of the originality of Taduno's talent. When he finished, TK began to applaud with a big smile on his face. The first set of studio staff were just starting to arrive, and seeing TK clapping they joined in, certain that he had discovered a prodigious talent. Soon, the whole corridor became filled with applause. And the legend of Taduno was born.

Taduno and TK established a great friendship and together made music that resounded in every corner of the country.

'We're almost there,' Aroli said. 'We're almost at the studio.' And then, glancing at Taduno, and seeing that he was smiling, he asked, 'Why are you smiling?'

The smile on Taduno's face broadened. 'Because we are almost there,' he replied.

*

He could sense that the air in the studio was different as he and Aroli walked in. It was not the same place he had walked into that June morning, almost twenty years ago. It was as if something had died there that was once alive.

The studio offices were situated on either side of a long corridor. The first door to the right was the reception – that had not changed. To the left, the waiting room – that had not changed. A security guard normally patrolled the corridor, directing visitors to the reception. But there was no security guard in the corridor at that moment, and Taduno took the impulsive decision to ignore protocol. As they continued along the corridor, he noticed that a lot of restructuring had taken place. The corridor was no longer as brightly lit as it used to be, and offices had been reorganised. The office that used to be TK's was now marked Conference Room. They moved on, and came to a door marked Studio Manager.

Taduno took a deep breath wondering if, like the rest of the world, TK would have forgotten him. He adjusted his guitar across his shoulder; then he knocked softly on the door.

'Come in.' The voice behind the door was brisk – and it wasn't that of TK.

Taduno and Aroli went in cautiously.

'What do you want?' the man seated behind a huge desk demanded roughly when he looked up and saw their strange faces. 'How did you get to my office without my secretary informing me?'

'So sorry if we barged in,' Taduno said softly, 'we are friends of TK.'

That got the man's attention. 'TK?'

'Yes,' Taduno replied hopefully.

'TK is no longer here.'

'No longer here? He owns this studio.'

'He used to. Not any more. I own the studio now.' To prove his point, the man pointed to the nameplate on his desk which read 'Mr Player'.

'What happened?'

'TK got into trouble with the government,' Mr Player said. 'His biggest star was making trouble with government, so government came down hard on him. He was on the verge of losing everything. I saved him by buying the studio.'

'You saved him by buying the most precious thing in his life?'

'What can be more precious in life than life itself?' Mr Player asked with an ironic grin.

'Who's this star that got TK into trouble?' Taduno's voice was pained, knowing the answer that would follow.

'Nobody knows him now. In the beginning everyone knew him. Then he became a stupid radical who fought the government with his music. Can you imagine anyone fighting government with music?' Mr Player gave a small laugh. 'Well, government destroyed him completely, beyond recognition. Now no one knows him, not even the government.'

'And TK, what happened to him?'

'He became an alcoholic when the government came down on him. He lost his biggest star. His other artists deserted him. He could no longer cope. He began to spend his money on alcohol. He was going to lose the studio, so I bought it from him.'

'Where can we find him?' Aroli asked.

'I cannot help you with that. I learned that he lost his house and became homeless. If you will take your leave now, I have important business to attend to.'

Taduno could not hide his dismay. He stammered words even he could not understand.

Aroli thought fast. 'You may be interested to know that my friend here is the biggest-selling star of all time,' he spoke in a rush, hoping they could salvage something from their visit.

'I don't know him,' Mr Player said, without interest.

'His name is Taduno.'

'I don't know him.'

'That's because he died and came back to life.'

Mr Player sat up behind his desk. 'Died and came back to life?' His eyes grew round with fear.

Taduno was too stunned to utter a word.

'Yes,' Aroli said, a serious expression on his face. 'Maybe if he plays his guitar you'll remember him.'

Mr Player hesitated, not sure if he wanted to hear the music of a man back from the dead.

Aroli capitalised on his hesitation. He nudged Taduno. 'Go ahead, play your guitar!'

But Taduno was too deflated to comply. He turned and walked out of the room. Aroli hurried after him. 'Think of Lela!' he pleaded. 'We must explore every opportunity that comes our way, for her sake.'

Out in the street, Taduno paused to catch his breath, his eyes moist with tears.

'The studio was the most precious thing in his life; that man took it away from him.'

'You heard his explanation. TK was going to lose it.'

'He took it away and gave him money for more booze, to complete his destruction.'

Aroli was lost for words.

'And I was the one who brought ruin upon him. I was the star who made trouble with the government.'

*

On the taxi ride back home they were silent, deflated. Taduno wondered if there was any hope for him, Lela or

TK. Aroli wondered if he and his neighbours would ever remember all they had forgotten. He was certain now that they, not Taduno, were the ones who forgot. A shiver ran through him.

Back at Taduno's place, they sat in the living room, each nursing a bottle of beer.

'I have to find him.' Taduno spoke suddenly.

'Find who?' Aroli's face creased into a frown.

'TK. Somehow, I believe he would remember me.'

'Why do you think he would remember you?'

'Because we have both suffered and lost so much. You don't forget when you have suffered and lost so much.'

'Even if he remembers you how will that secure Lela's release?'

'We need each other. If I find him we will be able to inspire each other. I will inspire him to produce again, and he will inspire me to sing again. I must find him!' He was charged with excitement now.

'Where are you going to start? He no longer works in the studio. And according to Mr Player, he lost his house.'

'That's where I will start, where he used to live. Someone will know something about him, surely.'

'Lagos is a very big city,' Aroli warned.

'Meaning what?' Taduno queried.

'Homeless people are often known to wander far away from the place they know as home.'

Taduno did not respond. He placed his face in his moist palms. Remaining like that for several minutes, he made up his mind to search the whole world for TK if he had to.

SEVEN

TK used to live in the lively neighbourhood of Ilasa, on a street where everyone knew everyone. An old record shop located at one end of the street played loud music, and from sunrise until midnight the music drove everyone at a fast pace through their daily activities.

The area boys moved through the street in tune to energetic music, picking the pockets of visitors, starting and quelling fights and generally running the affairs of the street, not with justice or fairness but with their fists, and on occasion with guns and knives.

While the street had no peace, it did have music, and it was that which made it special in the hearts of the residents. It was the music that persuaded TK to continue to live there many years after he became rich enough to live in a more affluent part of the city. Being a successful man who knew the true meaning of poverty, he continued to live on the street where he was born, to the disbelief of his business associates and the irritation of his many pretty female companions.

TK was a legend on the street, loved by everyone, even the area boys. He lived a simple life, and shared freely. For a man of his stature and wealth, many could not understand why he was content to drive a rickety Peugeot of no distinct model. He disliked designer clothes, and was always dressed in jeans and colourful *buba* tops, the exact manner he was dressed the day Taduno first ran into him in the brightly lit corridor of the studio that now belonged to Mr Player.

Taduno had been a regular visitor to the street in the past, and he was always well received. They all loved his music, because it enriched their lives with hopeful messages.

*

The record shop at the end of the street was still playing loud music the afternoon Taduno got there in search of TK. He had chosen to go there without Aroli because he considered the quest to find TK a personal business.

The area boys watched him suspiciously; in fact, everyone on the street picked up his scent. They were intrigued by this visitor who carried a guitar across his shoulder. And they knew without being told that he was looking for TK. They were somewhat surprised because no one had come looking for TK in a long time. When he lost his home and wandered away from that street, a string of pretty women had come looking for him in the first month, asking his neighbours if he had moved to a more affluent area. The women received rude responses, and they stopped coming after a while. Now a stranger carrying a guitar had shown up looking for a man that was no longer a part of their lives.

The pace of activity slowed down as Taduno walked down the street. He could make out several faces he knew, but there wasn't any hint of recognition in their eyes – they just stared at him with the hostility reserved for strangers.

When he stopped in front of a block of flats where TK used to live, the noises on the street and the music from the record shop died, as if a switch had been used to turn them off.

He greeted a young woman who was selling oranges in front of the block. She responded with a blank look on her tired, pretty face. She had been selling oranges at that same spot for years. Taduno knew her and had bought oranges from her a number of times, paying her generously on each occasion. She used to fondly refer to him as 'Oga Musisan' – 'Master Musician', a name she pronounced with a demure smile. He waited to see the light of recognition in her eyes, but they remained blank and suspicious, the way everyone looked at him the very first time he came to that street, before they knew he was a friend of TK's, before they knew he was the famous musician whose songs they played every day in their homes. Before they all became his friends – even the area boys – and they all began to call him Oga Musisan.

He reminded himself that he was now a man whose entire history had been erased from their minds. So he did not try to refresh the woman's memory. He knew full well that even if she remembered the name she had invented and made popular on the entire street, she would not remember his face as that of Oga Musisan. For a brief moment he closed his eyes in frustration.

'I'm looking for TK,' he said with a friendly smile. 'Where can I find him, please?'

Instead of responding to Taduno's question, the woman turned to the entire street and, raising her voice as loud as she could, announced in Yoruba: 'He is looking for TK ooo! I don't know where he came from ooo!'

*

A crowd of hostile faces promptly gathered around him; there wasn't a single friendly one among them. He turned this way and that way, and realised he was trapped.

He showed no fear, though. Somehow, the boldness in his eyes intimidated them. They stared curiously at his guitar, and they all thought it reminded them of someone, but they couldn't remember who.

'We understand you are looking for TK.' It was the coarse voice of a fierce-looking area boy.

'Yes, I'm looking for TK,' Taduno replied, turning to the thug who had addressed him. He knew the young man, a tall and bony individual who always hailed Oga Musisan with his fists in the air. Now he merely gave Taduno a blank look.

'TK no longer lives here. Who are you by the way? Where do you come from?'

'I'm a friend of TK's. Where can I find him?'

'We don't know where he lives. And we don't want him back here.'

Taduno was astounded at the words of the young man. They tore his heart.

'TK is a good man. He was a friend to you all. Why have you turned him into an enemy? Why?'

'Because we don't want any more trouble with gofment.'

'TK is not a troublemaker. He only produces good music.'

'TK and Oga Musisan were making trouble with gofment, and gofment came and beat everyone and arrested many of us, claiming that we were supporters of TK. They tortured us, and some people died in jail. Our people died in jail because of TK and Oga Musisan!'

Taduno was lost for words.

A bent old man stepped forward. He was bent not because of age but because of the years of suffering the city had heaped upon him.

The old man spoke with a thick drawl. 'TK's friend used to carry a guitar just like you. We all called him Oga Musisan. Now we don't remember his real name. We don't remember his face or anything about him. It sounds strange, but that is the truth. He used to make very good music in the beginning, but then he became a rascal, *omo ita*. How can any sensible person be rascal with gofment when gofment has guns and bombs? Can anyone be more rascal than gofment? TK and his friend failed to use their common sense, and they brought us grief when all we wanted was to live the way we have been living all of our lives.' The old man shook his head sadly.

He continued. 'And now you have come with your

guitar looking for TK. We don't have anything to do with TK any more, and we don't want anything to do with you and your guitar. When you find TK pass our message to him. We want to live our lives in peace, not pieces.'

Taduno turned slowly to look at the faces surrounding him. Faces of people TK had been kind to. He paid school fees for many of their children. He paid their hospital bills, their rent arrears, and even their debts to rich, wicked neighbours. He shared his food with them so that no one went hungry on that street. And now they had all betrayed him.

Taduno struggled to hold back his tears. He felt pained for the people, for their ignorance. He felt ashamed for them.

'TK was good to all of you. You betrayed him, you drove him away from your midst. How could you do that?' Taduno's voice was a whisper.

'Go away before we report you to gofment!' somebody shouted.

In response, Taduno unslung his guitar, and began to play a sad feathery tune. He did not need to sing. His guitar sang his song for him. It told the story of a man who loved his people so dearly he lived his life for them, shared their pains with them and gave them the joys and riches that abounded in his life. And then the people betrayed him and drove him away from their midst to roam the ruins of the city. Taduno's music rose in volume until it resounded throughout the length and breadth of that street.

The music pierced the souls of all that heard it, like

spears, even the hardened area boys. They retreated from him, their palms over their ears in agony, but nothing could stop the music from stirring their conscience. Some ran into their homes and locked their doors. But still the music found its way in. They lamented in loud voices like lunatics. They flung themselves on the floor and knocked their heads against walls until they began to bleed. They knew that they had committed mortal wickedness against a man who had showed them nothing but compassion.

*

By the time he ended his music, only one of the residents of that street remained – Baba *Ajo*, the man who had warned the rest of his neighbours to no avail not to pay TK evil for all the good he had done them. He wore the saddest face Taduno had ever seen.

So badly had Taduno's music tortured the conscience of the people of that street that none of them ventured out of their homes even after the music ended. The orange seller had left her precious oranges behind and would not come out to get them while Taduno remained on the street.

'I warned them,' Baba *Ajo* spoke quietly, struggling to control his emotions. 'I warned them, but they wouldn't listen to me.'

Taduno remembered the man. His son was once involved in a ghastly accident. TK paid the hospital bill, without which the boy's leg would have been amputated.

'Do you recognise me?' Taduno asked.

The man studied Taduno's face. Then he shook his head

slowly. 'No,' he said with a frown. A frown that said 'your face is familiar but I cannot remember where I have seen it before'.

Taduno sighed.

'Where can I find TK?'

'TK no longer remains in one place. He roams the city. Some say he spends a lot of time at TBS. Others say they have seen him at Mile 2, Oshodi and so on.'

'Has anyone come looking for him recently?'

'No, they stopped coming many months ago. At first a lot of his women friends came looking for him. They wanted to know if he had moved to a bigger and better house, but my neighbours chased them away. So they stopped coming.'

Taduno groaned quietly.

Baba *Ajo* continued. 'When you find TK please tell him I tried my best but they wouldn't listen to me. Tell him I'm sorry for all that happened to him. My name is Baba *Ajo*.'

'I know you. Your son once had an accident. He was to have his leg amputated, but TK made sure he got the treatment that saved his leg.'

The man could not hide his surprise. 'Who are you?'

'Like TK, I used to be a friend to you all. But I guess not any more. If I were to tell you who I am you will not believe me, you will only get confused.'

'Any friend of TK is my friend. You are my friend.' There was an eagerness about the man that showed how much he wanted to express his friendship for TK.

'I will give him your message when I find him.'

'I pray you find him. He was a good man who did not

deserve to be betrayed. They took side with gofment against TK. Where was gofment when TK was helping us? Where was gofment?' The questions left a pang in both their hearts.

Taduno thanked him and made his way from that street the way he came – slowly, with his guitar across his shoulder.

*

He narrated his experience to Aroli in a quiet mood. He felt pained not just because of TK's ordeal, but also because he knew how much he loved his less privileged neighbours. How much he used to care for them. How he used to take their pains as his own. How he saw their plight as his own. How he gave them hope. 'Yet they betrayed him so cruelly!' he lamented.

Aroli shook his head in dejection.

Later that evening, Judah paid him a visit. The boy listened to him playing his guitar for a while. But they both looked forlorn because the music he played that evening told sad stories. Although he longed to, he could not lift the boy's spirit with a beautiful song.

EIGHT

He was very anxious when he woke up the following morning, and his anxiety drove him through the city in search of the prodigious music producer turned homeless destitute. He travelled on one rickety bus after the other, with his guitar across his shoulder, a forlorn figure, searching the faces around him, hoping for a miracle.

Many stared at him, wondering why his guitar hung on his shoulder so awkwardly. Others wondered why his eyes were so expectant, yet so hopeless. A few gazed upon him with pity sensing that he bore a pain too intimate to be shared with the world.

At Mile 2 bus stop, and then Oshodi, he jostled amongst commuters who spoke in so many tongues. They spoke in Ibo, in Yoruba, in Hausa and in a hundred other tongues. It was as if people from all tribes of the country had converged at the bus stops on the occasion of his epic search. He was looking for a short man with Afro cut. And as he searched the faces at the bus stops, he was amazed how many such people there were in the city. At TBS, the square where a motley crowd gathered every day to see nothing in particular, he peered at the face of every beggar who bore the slightest resemblance to TK. He roamed the square until he became faint with hunger; yet still his tired feet carried him on. Night fell, and as the crowd waned, a gentle breeze lifted the square, drying the sweat from the faces and bodies of the homeless men who now remained.

For a while Taduno sat down to rest. Then he resumed his tour of the square with renewed energy, peering into every face more closely, knowing that the man he sought belonged to the small group that now remained. He drew angry responses as he went along. Some of the men raised their fists in warning, others lashed out at him with their legs; but the threats were not enough to deter him. He continued until he had gone round the square and stared into fifty or so faces.

In the end he collapsed on a wooden bench. And with his last ounce of strength, he unslung his guitar and began to play a forlorn tune that found its way into the hearts of all the men in that square. Gradually, they gathered around him, and they huddled together as one, knowing that the music they were hearing was a tribute to all their woes.

*

It was almost midnight when he began to make his way from the square towards the bus stop where the tired voices of bus conductors screamed various destinations. One of the homeless men trailed him. Taduno thought he was about to be mugged. Still some way from the bus stop, he hastened his steps, but the man soon caught up with him.

'Excuse me, please.' The voice lacked energy.

'Yes?'

'Who is it you are looking for?' the man queried, in a quite educated voice.

Taduno hesitated, surprised that the man spoke such good English. 'An old friend of mine,' he replied.

'The one for whom you played your guitar?'

'Yes.' Taduno relaxed, seeing that the man was not out to mug him. 'His name is TK.'

'TK, the music producer?'

Taduno stopped in his stride and turned to face the man. 'You know TK?' He was awash with excitement.

'Yes, I know him.'

'And who are you?'

'I'm nobody, just a homeless man.'

Taduno looked away.

'And you say you know TK?'

'Oh yes. He slept at the square with the rest of us last night.'

'He did?'

'Yes, he did. He comes and goes. I didn't see him today, but I'm sure he will come back. Come again tomorrow, and bring your guitar with you. Your music is very good.'

Taduno nodded. 'Thank you.'

He tipped the man some money. Then he continued to the bus stop, stopping once to look back.

*

He slept on the bus, until the voice of a twelve-year-old conductor woke him up at his stop. He got off the bus with his guitar dangling from his back.

It was an unusually quiet night; he saw no one about. He walked in quick long strides, slowing down when he got to his street. As he walked down the deserted street, accompanied by the echoes of his own footsteps, he noted that there were one or two houses still with lights on, and he suspected that somebody was watching him. At first he thought that somebody was Aroli, but he soon sensed that the eyes watching him were those of an unfriendly stranger and he became tense with fear. He threw quick looks over his shoulder to be sure no one was following him. Then he jogged the remaining distance to his house.

It wasn't until he was in the safety of his house that he began to relax. Without turning the light on he went to the window, up in his rehearsal room, and he parted the curtains slightly and peeped into the street. He did not detect any movement, but he knew, without any shadow of doubt, that somebody was out there.

His fear was confirmed the following morning when Aroli came banging on his door as early as seven o'clock; not with a smile on his face, but with a worried look.

'Where were you all day yesterday?' Aroli asked.

'Out searching for TK. Why do you look so worried?'

'A stranger came asking questions about you yesterday,' Aroli replied.

'Come, let's go upstairs,' he said hurriedly, and led Aroli to his rehearsal room.

'What did the stranger look like and what sort of questions did he ask?' He scrutinised Aroli's face in the same manner he had scrutinised the faces of the homeless men at TBS the previous night.

'Tall and broad-shouldered,' Aroli replied. 'He wanted to know about the relationship between you and TK. He didn't get any useful information, though.'

Suddenly Taduno understood. He let out a deep sigh.

'Somebody must have reported to the authorities,' he said. 'It could be any of TK's neighbours. They warned me that they don't want any more trouble with the government.'

'But how did the stranger manage to trace you here?'

Taduno rubbed his chin thoughtfully. 'He must have conducted his enquiries well.'

Aroli's face creased into a frown. He looked away from Taduno. 'I understand the man questioned Lela's parents, and even Judah. Everyone thinks he is secret service, and they're all getting worried. I think you should stop going about with your guitar. Nobody wants any trouble with government here either.' He turned to look at the guitar in a corner of the room.

'I don't think that is wise. It's clear they are already watching me. If I stop going about with my guitar that would tell them that I'm trying to hide something.'

'And if you keep going about with your guitar they'll keep following you and asking questions about you. And the neighbours will begin to see you as trouble. And they could decide to evict you.'

'But this is my house! I bought it with my own money, in my own name!' Taduno sounded desperate.

'Only you know that . . .' Aroli hesitated, 'and probably me. Remember, you once mentioned to me that you no longer have the documents to show you own the house.'

Taduno remembered Lela's warning and fear crept into his eyes. 'What will happen to Lela if I get arrested?' he lamented.

'We must avoid that until you discover your voice. Your voice is your identity, it is your bargaining power.'

'I must find TK urgently.'

'Find him. But stop going about with your guitar.'

He detected a trace of hostility in Aroli's voice. He threw him a sharp look. Aroli was the only person who knew his secret. He wondered if he would betray him. After Aroli had left, he went to check his mailbox. Only the letter he had written to Lela was there.

*

That morning heightened his fear.

Judah came to warn him too. 'You must be very careful, Uncle Taduno. A stranger came to ask questions about you yesterday. Everyone thinks he is secret service. But nobody knows why he is interested in you.'

'Thanks for letting me know. Aroli told me about it earlier.' He looked away so that the boy would not see the troubled expression on his face.

'I'm sure Uncle Aroli must have told you. I thought I should come to tell you also, so that you will take more care.'

Taduno nodded. 'Thank you. I will be more careful, and there is nothing to worry about.' He turned to the boy with a reassuring smile.

*

Refusing to take Aroli's advice, he went out with his guitar that morning and extended his search to all the popular bus stops in Lagos. Some of the people he talked to knew TK, but no one had seen him anywhere that day.

To his alarm, he discovered that there were many more policemen and soldiers than usual on the streets. They trained their guns on everyone, waiting to release fire at the slightest excuse. He wondered if the presence of the uniformed men had anything to do with him, or if the government was about to declare a state of emergency. He wondered if the man from secret service was on his trail.

As he made his progress through the city he kept throwing furtive glances to see if anyone was showing unusual interest in him. Because he threw looks at everyone, everyone threw looks at him too. And they wondered at him, at his strange guitar that stirred their conscience in an inexplicable way.

*

His shirt and trousers were torn and soiled by the time he got to TBS by late evening. As usual, a mammoth crowd milled about without purpose. He moved this way and that way, searching faces until darkness fell and all that remained was the rump of the crowd. As on the previous night, a gentle breeze fanned the square.

He played his guitar for several hours, surrounded by the homeless men whose hearts he delighted with his music. He played with total concentration; with a passion that rolled back the years. A round of warm applause greeted him when his music came to an end. And then the applause died down, and night became still. Somehow, he knew he would find TK soon. But he was not prepared for the miracle that would follow.

*

One by one the homeless men began to disperse to their sleeping positions, thoroughly thrilled by the music they had heard, filled again with some sense of life and hope. Taduno had his eyes closed, savouring the night peace that had taken hold of the square.

Soon he could hear loud snoring as the men were felled by sleep, one after the other. He listened to their snoring with his eyes closed. He listened, imagining each one of them as they once were, before they became homeless; before they succumbed to drugs and booze; before they sank in the quicksand of their most precious dreams and became snorers in a public square.

It was a cold night. He wrapped his arms around himself. The snores of the public snorers got louder; still he imagined them.

He opened his eyes and discovered that one man remained seated next to him on the wooden bench. He did not bother to turn to look at the man. He spoke to him through the corner of his mouth.

'It's cold and late. You should get some sleep.'

There was a brief silence. Then the man spoke.

'I listened to your music, to the song of your guitar; and I waited to hear your voice, but it never came.' The voice was rich and strong, the breath smelled of whisky.

Taduno stiffened. He straightened up on the bench, but he was too terrified to turn to look at the man. He was too terrified to speak, lest he discover he was in a dream. He closed his eyes again and the snoring in the square invaded his senses even more; the snoring of lost men, once so rich with colourful dreams.

The man spoke again.

'Taduno, is it really you?'

And then Taduno turned to look at the man, and he reached out and touched him; and feeling his being, his essence, it dawned on him that it was TK indeed. He had on a green fedora that shaded most of his face, and he was dressed in his usual style.

'TK?' Taduno whispered, unable to believe his eyes.

Rising to their feet, they locked in tight embrace. The unwashed smells of TK pervaded Taduno's senses; but he did not mind. He dragged in the smells deeply, grateful for the miracle of that moment.

'You remember me?' he asked, after they pulled back from their embrace.

'Why would I forget you? How can I forget you?' TK asked, with a tired laugh.

'Because the whole world has forgotten me. I returned

from exile to discover that no one remembers anything about me.'

'The whole world may forget, but I can never forget.'

They resumed their seats.

'I'm really sorry about everything that happened to you,' Taduno spoke, unsure what to say.

'It's not your fault,' TK said quietly.

A brief silence followed.

'You're coming home with me. You can no longer live on the street.' Taduno's eyes were on the bag at TK's feet.

'I can't. I'll only cause you more trouble. I . . .'

But Taduno wouldn't listen to his protests.

NINE

They had an early breakfast, not long after TK had shaved and had a nice warm bath and changed into fresh clothes provided by Taduno; not the style of clothes TK would usually favour but far better than anything he had worn in months. And then they settled down in the living room to watch the news.

'Which channel would you prefer?' Taduno asked as he flicked with the remote control.

'No state TV, please,' TK said mildly.

'I know better than that.' Taduno laughed. He disliked state TV as much as TK, so he tuned to the independent station, Channel 4.

The main news was the heavy military presence all over the city. The grave newscaster confirmed that no one knew what was happening. 'The whole country is waiting for the President to make an announcement, possibly to declare a state of emergency,' she said. 'One man was shot earlier in the day for speaking out against the government at a bus stop. But that is no news.' She looked into the camera with urgent eyes. 'In the past dozens have been mowed down, and everyone expects many more to be mowed down once a state of emergency is declared. The masses are already gathering sticks and stones in anticipation, the only weapons they have to fight the government. The whole city is becoming tense, and the President is keeping everybody in suspense as usual.'

She ended her broadcast with the weather report. 'The temperature is expected to rise as high as forty degrees. The city will burn most of the day, but for those at TBS, a gentle breeze will lift to dry their sweat by nightfall.' She signed off with sad but hopeful eyes.

Aha! thought Taduno. That is why a mammoth crowd often gathered at the square, to wait for the gentle breeze that would dry their sweat. Aha! he thought again.

*

He had been bracing himself to break the news to TK, but he did not know exactly how to start. TK had met Lela on several occasions, and he wondered how he would take the news of her kidnap.

He cleared his throat. Not so loud as to scare TK, but loud enough to get his attention.

'They kidnapped Lela,' he said, looking away from TK, afraid to see the reaction on his face.

TK dropped his glass of water on the table. He fixed Taduno with a look of disbelief.

'Which Lela? Who kidnapped her?'

'The same Lela you know – my girlfriend. She wrote me a letter in exile. It prompted me to return home. I returned to discover that no one remembers me, and then they told me Lela had been arrested by government agents. I did a little investigation, and I learned that she was actually abducted, not arrested.' He decided not to tell TK about the most recent letter from Lela.

'Abducted by who, and why would they abduct her?'

He told TK the story from the beginning.

*

The time was getting past midday. The TV was still on, but neither of them paid any attention to it.

'I returned from exile not knowing what had happened to you,' Taduno explained, rounding up his story. 'I thought you were still at the studio, and I did not want to pay you a visit because I was afraid that, like the rest of the world, you would no longer remember me. But then it became clear that I must learn to sing again to secure Lela's release. So I went to your studio, and I learned you had sold it. I went to your house too. Baba *Ajo* told me all that happened. He said he did his best but they wouldn't listen to him.' Taduno spoke slowly, as if to give TK the opportunity to digest his every word.

'I was taken before the President after you went into exile,' TK said. 'He wanted me to produce you, but I told him I could not. He vowed that he would make sure I never made music again. After that, the process of my ruin was rapid. He put machinery in place that ensured my complete destruction. I lost the studio, and then I lost my house. I left with just one small bag. They took everything I had, the people I lived with all my life. They shared my clothes, everything. I tried to plead with them; they said I brought them too much shame and pain. I walked away, and I walked for two days afterwards, without sleep, trying to understand the wickedness of their hearts.

'For two days I had nothing but liquor. It helped me to dull my pain. It even helped me to understand things better. And then it became too much and it tipped me over. I thought I would never be able to live without a drink. And then you found me, and now I know I will never touch it again.'

Taduno nodded in support. He did not trust himself to speak, so he just nodded, in a manner that suggested that the worst was over, that all would be well.

During the long silence that followed, TK digested all he had heard while Taduno reviewed all he had recounted, wondering if there was anything he had left out. As yesterday and today became connected by the slowly uncoiling thread of memory, they remembered all their hopes and dreams for tomorrow. Eventually they returned to the present. And when TK spoke, it was with a thoughtfulness born out of the silence that had passed.

'Listen to me, Taduno,' TK spoke softly. 'Please listen very carefully.'

Taduno sat up. 'Yes,' he said.

'We are going to make beautiful music together again.'

Taduno nodded eagerly. 'Yes.'

'But we are not going to praise-sing. You cannot make

beautiful music by praise-singing. You cannot use beautiful music to praise-sing.'

'The life of the woman I love is at stake,' Taduno said with dismay.

'The government wants you to support it with your music. But I tell you, if you do that you are as good as dead. They will use you then they will silence you.'

'If I don't they will kill Lela.'

'No, they will not,' TK said confidently.

'The Sergeant said they will kill her if I refuse to praise the government with my music.'

'They have to find you first. I mean, they have to remember you first. Whatever!' He placed a palm on his temple. 'From what you told me, nobody remembers you; nobody but me. They are holding Lela as a bargaining chip. They will not hurt her until they find you. They need you to praise the government with your song. I assure you Lela is very safe as we speak. In the meantime, let's focus on making beautiful music again. And then we can take on the government on our own terms.'

Taduno looked uncertain, but somehow felt comforted by TK's assurance that nothing bad would happen to Lela – until they found him.

*

Having wandered around the city most of that day trying to find a buyer for a multi-storey property, Aroli showed up while TK was sleeping in the guest room upstairs. Strangely, he knocked on the door quietly; so quietly

Taduno almost missed the sound of the knock. And when he opened the door and saw that it was Aroli, his heart skipped a beat. He wondered if he had come to give him away quietly to the authorities, without fuss, without any drama. Or was it possible that he knew that TK was in his house?

He had brought TK home under the cover of darkness, using the back door. And he felt certain that no one saw them come in. So why did Aroli come knocking so quietly, so unusually? Did he sense TK's larger-than-life presence?

They could both feel the tension in the air. Taduno did not know what to say; he felt uncomfortable knowing that TK was upstairs, and he wondered how Aroli would react when he found out.

'I came to see how you are doing,' Aroli said as he took a seat.

Taduno ignored his words. He made up his mind to tell him there and then. 'He's upstairs, sleeping,' he said, nodding towards the staircase.

'Who is upstairs?' Aroli asked with a frown.

'TK. I found him last night and brought him home sometime after midnight. He's upstairs sleeping.'

A groan emanated from Aroli's throat. 'Did anyone see you?' he asked.

'I don't think so, we came in through the back door. The entire neighbourhood appeared to be asleep then.'

'But they will know about his presence sooner or later. And when the man from the secret service turns up again they will tell him TK is here. And you know what that means.'

Taduno looked away. 'I couldn't leave him on the street. I had to bring him here.'

'You could have taken him elsewhere, not here.' There was fear in Aroli's voice. 'If the government gets to know that he is here it will bring everybody a lot of trouble. I can imagine what they will do to us. They will send in soldiers to kick all our arses. They will lock many of us up. They will destroy our properties, and rape our women. They will do a lot of nasty things to us, but I can't imagine what they will do to you and him. Have you thought about all that? Have you?'

'Nobody has to know that he is here,' Taduno said defensively. 'He'll remain indoors until we are able to work out a safer arrangement for him.' He began to walk round the living room in a widening circle, like a man in a trance.

'How long are you going to keep him indoors? How long? I'm sure you are going to be rehearsing together, trying to discover your voice again. That's not something you can do quietly. Very soon the neighbours will sense that he is here. And all our lives will change.'

'I need to have him here if I'm to recover my voice and save Lela. Please try to understand.'

'Of course I understand,' Aroli laughed bitterly. 'We're neck-deep in this together, you and me! But must we forget the pain we could end up causing the innocent people of this street?'

'I promise we'll keep things quiet,' Taduno pleaded. 'Before you know it he'll be out of here. It is just for a short while until he can find his own accommodation.' He laughed uncertainly. 'Hey, you might be able to help with that – getting TK affordable accommodation, I mean.'

In spite of himself, Aroli laughed. His laughter was warm; it dispelled Taduno's fears.

TEN

But they couldn't keep things quiet for long. As the days passed by and their rehearsal sessions became more intense, Taduno's neighbours began to suspect that something wasn't quite right. They were used to hearing only the music of his guitar, but now a croaky voice accompanied that music. And as the voice underwent a painfully slow improvement day after day, they began to gather beneath the upper-room window once again to marvel at the music of his guitar and the voice that got better and better.

They soon discovered that there were two voices at work in that upper room that had now become a part of the great mystery that joined them to him: one voice issuing instructions, the other undertaking the painstaking task of singing. They wondered if he now dwelled with a ghost. They wondered, too, what sort of music they were trying to make, if the music would change their lives.

The neighbours spent more and more time beneath the

upper-room window, and Aroli devoted himself more and more to his work as an estate agent, pursuing bigger deals and enduring longer hours of frustration – all in an effort to spend more time away from the street.

The people could not understand by what miracle the croak of a voice was being transformed. Some said that the ghost had taken over the singing; others said Taduno had become a ghost too, and his voice was now that of an ethereal being. Everyone forgot that the man from the secret service promised to come back.

*

Sensing that Taduno was getting more consumed with his music, Judah began to visit him less frequently, not wanting to be obtrusive. He understood that Taduno must discover his voice in order to find his sister. On the occasions the boy visited, he noticed that Taduno kept looking at the stairs leading to the upper room. He assumed that it was because he was eager to get back to work; he never suspected that TK was up there, waiting for the all clear.

And so the boy would make his visits very brief. 'I know you must get back to work,' he would say. 'The earlier you discover your voice, the better. Maybe it will help us to remember you.'

Taduno would smile with a hint of guilt. Often, he thrilled the boy with a beautiful song before saying goodbye.

*

One afternoon, without thinking of Taduno's warnings, TK parted the curtains of a window in the upper room to get a bit of fresh air and some sun. As he stretched by the window, he realised that the entire street was gathered below. But it was too late for him to pull the curtains together. The people stared up at him. And as they beheld the Afro cut that graced his face like a halo, they gave a collective gasp, and it dawned on them that the man above was TK, the famous music producer. A second gasp rose from the crowd, and they fled, certain that their lives were about to be altered for ever.

Taduno had gone downstairs to get some water. He returned to discover that TK's cover was blown. All he could do was mutter a silent prayer.

*

Maybe it was that prayer that summoned Aroli back at that particular time. As soon as he disembarked from an *okada*, the entire street rushed to meet him, to share their discovery.

'He has him in his house.' 'We saw him, he came to the window.' 'They have been making music together all this while.' 'He is the man the secret service man came to enquire about.' Their voices clashed as they all tried to speak at once.

Aroli felt deflated. He had always known it would happen sooner or later. And now that it had happened, he wondered what would follow.

'Okay!' he said, raising his voice and his hand for quiet. 'Let's not bring down the tower of Babel.'

Everyone became quiet. None of them liked the sound of bringing down the tower of Babel.

'Who are we talking about here?' Aroli asked.

Looking round at their faces, Aroli saw their fear, their confusion, and he felt pained that he had allowed this to come upon them. However, he reminded himself that he had to get the situation under control, or else all would be lost.

'What did you see? Who are you talking about?' Aroli pressed, even though he knew the answers to his questions.

The big man known as Vulcaniser, who owned a road-side workshop on the street, cleared his throat to indicate that he wanted to speak.

'Please speak,' Aroli said, nodding towards the man.

Vulcaniser cleared his throat again in further warning, a man who understood that you could never be too careful, especially when the issue was as serious as that at hand. He rubbed a palm across his face. Then he took a few paces through the small crowd towards Aroli.

'We saw TK, the music producer, upstairs in Taduno's house. He came to the window. They have been making music together all this while.' Vulcaniser's voice was taut.

For a moment, Aroli was lost for words.

'Are you sure he was the one you saw?'

'Very sure,' Vulcaniser responded. 'He is a popular man, everybody knows him.' He spread out his hands to show his point as the others nodded in agreement.

'So what's the issue?' Aroli asked, pretending not to know.

'The man from the secret service said he would come

back. He warned us not to withhold any information we have about TK. He said we would face grievous punishment if we did.'

'And he promised us a big reward of money if we supplied useful information about TK,' one man spoke from the back of the crowd.

'Shh!' Vulcaniser said in loud warning. 'Let's not bring down the *towel of banbel*. Speak only when you are asked to speak.'

'Thank you,' Aroli said, appreciating Vulcaniser's effort to maintain order. 'So what must we do now?'

'I think we should tell the secret service man everything we saw when he comes back.'

Aroli reflected for a moment.

'I don't think that's the best solution to the problem. Remember, the man from the secret service works for government. And government never keeps a promise. I can tell you that if you report this matter, you won't get any monetary reward. Instead, they'll beat everyone and lock everyone up. I'm sure you all have an idea what a government cell looks like. So I say we should just keep this matter between ourselves as neighbours.'

Their voices broke out again, and they argued amongst themselves. And they spoke in anger because they were afraid and no one agreed with anyone else. They spoke like this for almost a minute until Aroli raised his voice above all theirs.

'Remember the tower of Babel!' he shouted.

Quiet instantly returned. Sweat dripped down all their faces, and they began to shake, confused about what to do; uncertain what would happen to them if they did what they had to do or if they failed to do what they must do. They all looked to Aroli for direction. And the direction he gave them was a simple one – each one of them must keep their mouths shut about what they had seen.

*

Aroli came face to face with TK for the first time since he moved in with Taduno. Actually, it was the first time he had ever seen TK in the flesh, and he was amazed at his magnetic personality. He wore a simple smile; his Afro cut was dark and well kept.

Aroli greeted TK in a reverent manner, shaking his hand as if to say 'I've always wanted to meet you!'

TK's handshake was warm, and it passed a current between them that came from the depth of his being. Several minutes after that handshake, Aroli still felt his touch, and he kept looking at the man and then down at his own hand, wondering if he had touched him with magical light.

In Taduno's living room, the three men discussed the development on that street.

'They all know that TK is here,' Aroli said, as if TK was not in the room with them.

'It was a mistake,' Taduno explained in a tired voice. 'TK wasn't aware that they were outside the window. He forgot my warning that they could be watching us.'

'They thought of reporting it to the secret service man next time he turns up,' Aroli said. 'But I talked them out of it.'

'I think I should leave,' TK said, rising to his feet.

'No!' Aroli said sharply. 'You don't have to. You have nowhere to go. I'm hopeful that they will keep their mouths shut. Stay, please. But be more careful next time.'

'Thank you, Aroli,' Taduno said, looking away. To think that he had been afraid that Aroli would betray him. He suddenly felt ashamed.

'Please sit down, TK,' Aroli implored.

TK remained standing.

'Please sit down, TK,' Taduno added.

For a moment, TK studied both their faces; then he resumed his seat. 'I don't want to bring trouble to folks around here,' he said quietly.

'Think about it,' Aroli said. 'If they report your presence everyone will get into trouble for sure. They are better off keeping their mouths shut, and that's what I told them. Concentrate on making beautiful music again and then we'll take it from there.'

'How much does he know?' TK asked Taduno, nodding towards Aroli.

'He believes my story even though he cannot remember me,' Taduno explained. 'He believes that they are the ones who forgot the past and everything about me.'

TK shook his head. 'I have never seen so much faith,' he muttered under his breath.

ELEVEN

The man from the secret service turned up the following afternoon. From the buzz on the street, Taduno had advance warning, so he told TK to hide in the attic amongst several sturdy shelves where it would be difficult to find him. And then he went to sit in the living room with his guitar, waiting to hear a knock on his door.

The knock came about an hour after the secret service man arrived on the street, after he had visited all the other houses to ask questions. Taduno went to open the door holding his guitar in one hand. He knew that his fate was no longer in his own hands but in the hands of neighbours who did not remember a thing about him.

He invited the man in politely. He noted that he was tall and broad-shouldered, with a very quiet demeanour. He offered him a comfortable seat. He offered him cold water in a large mug. He had learned from somewhere that men like him who worked for government were always thirsty and hungry. But he had no food to offer him, and he dearly wished he had some food in the house, a piece of chicken maybe.

He waited for the man to drain the contents of the mug, and then he asked him if he wanted more. The man nodded, and he went and got him more water, in a bigger mug. And as the man nursed the mug of water in his hand, Taduno asked, 'To what do I owe this visit?'

'You seem like a very nice person,' the man observed.

'Thanks for the compliment. By the way, my name is Taduno. What's yours?'

The man gave a wry smile.

'My name is irrelevant. Names are irrelevant in my line of work. You can simply refer to me as the man from the secret service.'

Taduno nodded. 'It makes a lot of sense,' he said, even though it made no sense to him at all.

'Thanks for the water,' the man said with a smack of his lips. 'That was very cold. The best cold water I've tasted in a while.'

Taduno nodded. 'You're welcome.' He did not ask if he wanted more.

'As I was saying, you seem like a really nice person. I don't know why government is showing a sudden interest in you.' He paused. 'Oh yes, it has to do with TK, of course. My bosses want to know the connection between the two of you. I understand you've been going around with your guitar making enquiries about TK. Correct?'

'Correct,' Taduno nodded.

'If you don't mind me asking, is that the same guitar

you've been going around with?' He pointed at the guitar in Taduno's hand.

'Yes,' Taduno replied.

'You see, I'm asking these questions so that I'll know what to report back to my bosses. So please don't think that any question is unnecessary.'

Taduno nodded. 'I understand completely.'

'When and where did you buy the guitar in question?'

Taduno thought for a moment. He decided to answer the question truthfully.

'I bought it some weeks back,' he replied, 'from a second-hand shop in Tejuosho market.'

'Do you have a receipt for it?'

'Oh yes, I do. I can get it if you want.'

The man waved that away. 'Never mind, it won't be necessary, so long as you have a receipt.'

'Yes, I do,' Taduno said helpfully.

'Now let's talk about TK.'

'What about him?'

'Why have you been going around with your guitar looking for TK?'

'TK is an old friend. I haven't seen him for some time, so I thought I should pay him a visit.'

'And is that why you've been going round bus stops all over the city asking questions about him? You want to pay him a visit at the bus stop?'

Taduno wished the questioning would come to an end.

'Well, nobody knows his whereabouts, so I decided to extend my search all over the city.'

'And what have you discovered? Have you found him or heard anything about him?'

'No, nothing at all,' he responded, fixing his eyes on the secret service man.

The man asked a few more questions. Then he nodded, satisfied, pausing for a while, as if going over a mental note. He tapped the side of his head with one finger and then nodded again.

'Well, I guess that will do for now. If you find TK or hear anything about him, report to the nearest police station.' His voice had suddenly turned hard. He rose to leave. 'I'll keep in touch. Thanks again for the water. It was really cold!'

Taduno nodded with relief, dazed from answering so many seemingly stupid questions.

*

'It's just a matter of time before someone gives me away,' TK said, after the secret service man had left the street.

'Let's hope that does not happen. Aroli is working amongst them to make sure they keep their mouths shut. He has a way with people. I'm sure he will manage to keep them from talking.'

'He is a very interesting young man,' TK observed. 'I like him. He is direct.'

Taduno nodded. 'Yes, he is direct. But for a moment I almost thought he was being two-faced with me.'

'One shouldn't be too quick to judge.'

Later, Aroli brought them some food from Mama Iyabo's

restaurant, and some good news. He watched Taduno and TK eat, noting that they both ate in the same fashion – slowly, but with zest.

'You must join us,' Taduno said. 'The food's good.'

'Thanks, I've already had something to eat,' Aroli said, walking slowly round the living room. 'How's practice going?'

TK cleared his throat. 'Great. His voice has improved tremendously. He will soon be ready to sing again.'

Aroli rubbed his palms together. 'There's good news from the street. The neighbours are cooperating. I spoke to them individually, and they all gave me their word not to mention your presence to anyone. I wasn't around when the secret service man came earlier, but I understand that no one gave him any useful information.'

'He was here to see me,' Taduno said. 'We had a chat while TK was up in the attic. He seemed like a nice guy, but I know that his niceness is not real.'

They finished eating. While Taduno took the dishes to the kitchen, TK and Aroli chatted lightly.

'I understand you are a poet,' TK said, with a smile.

'Yes,' Aroli responded. 'But you see, poetry does not put food on my table, for now, so I make money as an estate agent.' His usual line. 'I can get you very affordable accommodation when you are ready. No agency fee, no legal fee! But you must give me three recommendations.'

'I see. And you'll make what you are losing to me from my recommendations, I presume?'

'You get it! Robbing Peter to pay Paul.'

They both laughed.

'That's very kind of you indeed,' TK said. 'Maybe I'll commission you to write some songs for me when I get back to producing music. Poets can be good songwriters.'

'I'd be delighted to write you some songs, seriously. But I hope song writing's not a poor art like poetry?'

'Find out when the time comes,' TK responded with a laugh.

*

It did not come as a shock to anyone when the President went on air to declare a state of emergency in Lagos. What did come as a shock to Taduno – and indeed everyone – was his reason for doing so. In a nationwide broadcast, the President explained that music had caused a lot of problems for his government in recent times. As a result, his government had decided to ban all association through music. He went on to explain that a certain music producer who had been on the government's radar had suddenly disappeared into thin air and he feared that this individual could go back to making troublesome music in an attempt to bring down his government. He urged everyone to cooperate with his security forces in their investigations, warning that anyone who failed to do so would be severely punished. In order to minimise the threat facing the nation, his government was imposing a dusk-to-dawn curfew in Lagos until further notice. Anyone found on the street during curfew hours would be shot like a dog, no, a goat, he corrected. He explained that goats are known to be very stubborn animals. So anyone who flouted the curfew would be shot like a goat.

He ended his broadcast with a charming smile.

'Long live the Federal Republic!' he said. 'May God bless us all.'

*

Protesters hit the streets the following morning, claiming the curfew was a violation of their human rights. They had sticks and stones to face heavily armed soldiers. They lit up tyres in the streets. The rapid sound of gunfire rang across the city, and anguish soon followed as protesters were felled in battle.

For a moment it crossed Taduno's mind to give up TK and put an end to the bloodshed. But he knew that TK would be shot like a goat if he was found. And the killing in the streets would continue all the same.

So he bore the pain. And so did TK and Aroli.

The three men sat miserably at a table in a corner of Taduno's living room, trying to figure out the best thing to do. But they came up with nothing, and the lopsided battle in the streets of Lagos continued.

*

In the afternoon, his neighbours gathered in Vulcaniser's compound to discuss the predicament of a city whose fate lay at their doorstep. They had a lengthy meeting, chaired by Aroli. They spoke quietly, fully aware that should the secret they harboured go beyond their street, a swarm of soldiers would descend on them, and that street would be completely erased from the city's map.

Vulcaniser reminded them that they must look to Aroli for direction. They must remain united, and they must guard their deadly secret jealously.

Everyone nodded their agreement.

The meeting was nearing an end when Taduno joined them. He saw raw fear and pain in their eyes, and guilt wrenched his heart. He had come to offer an apology, which he gave in a quivering voice. He begged their forgiveness for all the trouble he had brought upon them, indeed the entire city. They stared at him, silently, but without resentment, knowing he was a victim like the rest of them.

TWELVE

The secret on Taduno's street was leaked inadvertently when Lela's father went to see a friend. Because the mood everywhere was sombre, he did not knock on the door. Instead, he tiptoed into his friend's living room. And so he came upon a quiet discussion between man and wife about how long Taduno would continue to harbour TK.

By the time the man and his wife realised that there was an eavesdropper in their midst, it was too late. Lela's father already knew too much; he already knew that the cause of the city's woes lay in that street, at the doorstep of the stranger who entered their lives some weeks ago.

The man pleaded with Lela's father to keep all he heard secret, explaining that soldiers would raze the entire area if they found out the truth.

Lela's father nodded stiffly. 'I understand the gravity of the matter,' he said. 'I'll keep it to myself.'

He left after he shared a lobe of kolanut with his friend, his shoulders heavy with the secret he now carried.

Aroli saw him leaving the street in a hurry, and he knew that something wasn't right.

*

'I saw Lela's father leaving our street in a hurry,' Aroli told Taduno later.

'He must be rushing to get home before the start of curfew,' Taduno replied casually.

'No, there was something about his appearance I found very disturbing.'

'What?' Taduno gave him a questioning look.

Aroli ignored the question. 'Where is TK?' he asked.

'He is upstairs sleeping. He had a very rough time on the streets, he needs a lot more sleep these days.'

Aroli chewed his lips. 'Even though they gave me their word, we have to be ready for the possibility of betrayal.' He paused, a distant look in his eyes. 'I wonder if Lela's father has found out our secret somehow. Is it possible?'

Taduno did not respond. Instead, he began to pace the living room, his heart racing faster and faster.

'Do you think he has found out?' he asked.

'I'm worried by the way he left,' Aroli replied. 'He had his head down, and he kept throwing glances over his shoulder. I have no doubt he was getting away from some-thing. What could that be?'

'Who did he visit?' Taduno's voice was taut.

'I don't know. I could find out, but I'm afraid that it will raise tension on the street if I try to.'

'Better not to.'

Aroli nodded.

TK was still sleeping when Aroli took his leave. At the door, he said: 'Time is of the essence. You need to discover your voice soon.'

*

But Taduno was still a long way from singing. Even though his voice was much better, it was not yet the voice of the man the government was looking for. And so, while Lagos raged in battle, they continued their rehearsals quietly in the attic.

There were no soldiers on patrol on their street. A truckload of them had driven through two days earlier, throwing tear gas and shooting into the air. But it had been calm afterwards, even though the distant sound of gunfire and cries of agony continued. They could see thick smoke rising into the air across the city. And the hot wind deposited soot over their roofs and on their doorsteps.

In the following days, the President poured more soldiers into the city to quell the protests. After nearly two weeks of fierce fighting, the protesters pulled out of the streets and the battle ended.

Gradually, the city became quiet as the people mourned their dead. On Taduno's street, fear mixed with relief; no one had died there because none took part in the protests. And now that the battle had ended, they felt like traitors who had forced the city into war while they hung back and watched people die.

*

Many hours later, fires continued to burn, and soldiers covered in soot kept vigilant patrol. With their black helmets and torn boots, they looked like warriors left to take charge of a fallen city. The soldiers knew that as long as the fire remained, protesters could hit the streets in a surprise attack. So they kept their guns at the ready.

Lagos truly had fallen. The protesters refused to return to the streets. Too many of their own had died in battle. 'Maybe we shouldn't have taken up arms against the government,' they wailed. In their anguish, they realised that the dictator had them exactly where he wanted.

The grave-looking Channel 4 newscaster caught the mood of the city. In her words: 'The battle has been lost and won. And now the people must get on with their lives. But will they ever enjoy any semblance of normality again?'

She signed off with a sad smile. There was no one in the city who could save it from tyranny.

*

Two days later, the President lifted the curfew and pulled most of the soldiers off the streets, but many of Taduno's neighbours were still too scared to venture out of their homes. They spent long hours watching the street from their windows, wondering if the secret service man would return, or if soldiers would invade their homes to arrest them.

That morning, while TK used the bathroom, it occurred to Taduno that he had not checked his post in days, so he went outside to check his mailbox. To his surprise, he discovered two brown envelopes: a new letter from Lela, and his own to her, which had remained there ever since. For a few moments he was transfixed. And then, trembling with excitement, he hurried inside with the letter from Lela. He went upstairs and locked himself in his bathroom so that TK would not stumble upon him reading it. He touched the envelope to his lips in appreciation of Lela's pain and the sacrifice she was making for him. And then, taking out the letter, he began to read.

— — —

Dear Taduno,

I hope you are well. I have lost count of the days in here, and nothing makes sense to me any more. I wish I could get out of this nightmare by opening and closing my eyes. But each time I try, the reality gets more depressing.

I look forward to the day I will be back in your arms. Sometimes I hear your voice singing to me, and I'm hopeful that you will get me out one day.

I don't know what is happening to my parents and Judah. I miss them so much. I hope Judah is OK, and I pray that he wasn't arrested too.

I would love to get back to the classroom. In here, I

*have come to realise that the affection I have for my
students is more important than the equations I teach
them.*

*I wonder if I will ever taste freedom again . . . You
remain my only hope.*

Love you always,

Lela

He sat in the bathroom for some time, running the tap to
drown his tears and sorrow. Then he washed his face,
dabbing it with a towel. In the mirror, his eyes were dead
and red.

After hiding the letter in the same place as the last one,
he returned downstairs to find TK and Aroli in a quiet
discussion. A knock came on the door just then. Taduno
delayed; enough for TK to hide up in the attic. Aroli
whispered something inaudible. And then Taduno opened
the door, and they were both relieved to see that the visitor
was Judah.

'Hello, Judah!' Taduno exclaimed. 'How are you? Come
in, please.' Noticing the sadness on the boy's face, he asked,
'What's the matter?'

'I had to come without letting my parents know,' the
boy replied.

'Please sit down. Are you okay? Is there a problem? Tell
me, please.'

The boy sat down, but remained quiet.

'Can I get you something to drink, some water maybe?'
Taduno asked, smiling broadly at the boy.

'No, thank you. I don't need anything to drink. I need

to talk to you.' The fear in the boy's eyes grew as he looked from Taduno to Aroli.

'What's the matter?' Taduno squatted in front of Judah. 'What is it you need to talk about?'

The boy hesitated and scratched his cheek, averting his eyes.

'Look at me, Judah.' Taduno smiled. 'You can tell me anything you want to tell me. Do not be afraid. Go ahead, please.' He reached out and patted the boy lightly on the shoulder to encourage him.

'You promised you would find my sister,' the boy began uncertainly.

'Yes, I promised. I will find your sister.' Taduno nodded reassuringly.

'But I overheard my parents discussing . . .' Again the boy hesitated.

'What were they discussing?'

'They were discussing you . . . you and TK.' The boy swallowed nervously. 'My father said TK is in your house. He wants to tell the police. He said he will get a lot of money for the information. My mother agreed. My father wants to go the police, but my mother wants him to wait for the man from the secret service.' Judah began to cry, knowing he had betrayed his parents.

Taduno and Aroli exchanged glances. Aroli shook his head in dejection.

A feeling of hopelessness overcame Taduno. He felt sad that his effort to save the woman he loved was about to be frustrated by her own parents. And he felt sorry for the boy, for the cruel burden his parents had placed on him.

'Stop crying, please,' he said to him, shaking him gently by the shoulder. 'Don't cry. You are so kind for coming to tell me, and I'm grateful.'

'I'm afraid,' Judah said, wiping his eyes with the back of his hands.

'Don't be afraid. Please stop crying.'

'I'm afraid that if you are arrested you will not find my sister again.'

'Don't worry. I will not be arrested, and I will find your sister. I promise, I will find her very soon.'

Taduno soothed the boy with his words. Then he got him a glass of water.

After the boy had finished drinking, Aroli asked, 'Has your father gone to the police station?'

'No, he agreed to wait for the secret service man. My mother wants to know how much money they will get.'

'And do you know if he has told anyone else what he knows, anyone apart from your mother?'

'I don't think so. He warned my mother not to tell anyone. He says if she does, he might lose the money.'

This last revelation came as a small relief to both men. Their secret was in the hands of a greedy man.

'Okay, I will see you home,' Aroli said, rising to his feet. 'Look, don't say anything to anyone about what you heard your parents discussing. And don't tell your parents you were here. If you do, it will make it difficult for Taduno to find your sister. Understand?'

'Okay.' Judah nodded, staring into Aroli's face.

'Let's go.' Opening the door, Aroli held out his hand to the boy.

The boy looked from one man to the other.

Taduno smiled at the boy.

The boy managed a smile too. And as he walked away in quick small strides beside Aroli, he wondered if God would forgive him for betraying his parents.

*

Aroli got back twenty minutes later to find Taduno and TK talking quietly in the living room. Without bothering to ask if either of them needed a drink, he went into the kitchen to get a bottle of beer. 'We have to do something,' he said, after he had taken a drink and settled into a seat. He kept his eyes on the bottle of beer in his hand.

'Do what?' Taduno asked.

'Do something about what Judah told us.'

'What can we do?'

'I don't know. Anything. Sooner or later, his father will report us to the secret service man or the police.' Aroli sounded nervous.

'I think what we can do is appeal to him not to go to the police, not to say anything to the man from the secret service. We could even pay him to keep quiet.' Taduno looked at Aroli, then TK.

'You cannot appeal to the conscience of a greedy man,' TK spoke. 'You cannot pay him enough either. His mind is set on the reward the government has promised. Nothing will change his mind. Even if you pay him, he will still want to get the extra from the government. I see only one solution – I must leave.'

'You cannot leave,' Taduno said hastily. 'You have nowhere to go.'

Aroli agreed. 'You cannot leave. The streets are deserted. If you go into the streets, they will pick you out easily. And I'm afraid they will not take you in alive.'

'Are you suggesting I wait for them to come and get me here?'

'No, I'm suggesting we do something else. Maybe we should kidnap the boy's father. We could keep him here until Taduno is able to sing again and in a position to negotiate with the government.' Aroli spoke in a rush.

'If we kidnap the man, his wife will go to the police. That will complicate the situation.' Taduno shook his head.

'She will not go to the police if we make her realise that her husband will die if she does. See?' Aroli said.

'We are not killing anyone.' Taduno's voice was sharp.

'Kidnappers are supposed to back up their actions with threats. We do not have to kill him.'

'We are no better than the government if we act in that way,' TK said, rising to his feet and leaning against the wall.

Taduno put up his hands. 'I agree. Think about it. Apart from the people on this street, who else knows that TK is here? There may be others. You cannot rule out the possibility. It could be that the secret is out. And if that is the case, kidnapping Judah's father will do no good.'

'I don't see a better way,' Aroli said stubbornly.

'I know a better way,' Taduno said, rising to his feet, 'I could stir the man's conscience with music.' He grabbed his guitar from a corner of the room with a sense of urgency.

108

'Come with me, Aroli! We've got no time to waste.' To TK, he said, 'Do not open the door for any reason. Go up to the attic and remain there until we come back.'

TK opened his mouth to say something, but only a deep sigh emerged. He knew now that his fate was in the hands of strangers.

THIRTEEN

They found Lela's parents at home, but there was no sign of Judah. The man and his wife welcomed them nervously and offered them cold water. They brought out kolanut too, in a blue plastic bowl. And then the wife disappeared to the backyard to eavesdrop on the ensuing conversation.

'To what do I owe this visit?' Lela's father asked, after his visitors had taken some water and politely declined the kolanut. He kept looking nervously at Taduno's guitar. He sensed that the guitar meant trouble, and he wished he hadn't come with it.

'Oh, we just came to visit you as neighbours,' Taduno said. 'I am aware that I haven't paid you a proper visit since I returned.' He hesitated. 'I mean, since I moved to this neighbourhood.'

'It is very thoughtful of you to come,' Lela's father said, beginning to sweat profusely. 'I see Aroli around a lot. He is always riding through our street on *okada*.'

Aroli nodded eagerly. 'Oh yes, that is right.'

'By the way, where is Judah?' Taduno asked.

'I think he must be in his room sleeping.'

'I see.' Taduno nodded, then hesitated. 'I'm sorry about your daughter. I understand she was arrested by government agents. How sad!' He shook his head.

The man became downcast. 'Oh yes, she was arrested many weeks ago. And we have not heard anything about her since. The police claim they don't know anything. Nobody knows anything. It is a shame that we live in a society like this.' He gave a small shrug.

'It is a shame indeed!' Taduno shook his head. 'But it may give you some consolation that Aroli and I are trying to find your daughter, and we have made considerable progress so far. Rest assured we will find her.'

A happy smile broke out on the man's face. 'Oh, that is very kind of you! I cannot thank you enough.'

'You don't have to. We should be there for each other as neighbours,' Taduno said, spreading out his hands.

There was a brief pause.

'And that is why we have come to see you,' Aroli said, straightening up in his seat.

And then Lela's father suddenly knew why they were there. But he could not understand how they knew. Is it possible that his wife betrayed him? He wiped sweat from his face with his palm.

'I'm listening.' His voice was a croak.

'I have TK, the man the government is looking for, in my house,' Taduno began. 'We understand that you are aware of this and that you intend to report to the authorities. If

111

you do that, Aroli and I will be arrested and we will no longer be able to find your daughter. So we are here to beg you to keep what you know to yourself.'

A long silence followed.

'There's a reward for the information. What do you expect me to do?' the man asked at last.

'We expect you to keep quiet!' Aroli said in a tough voice. He wanted to add 'or we will kidnap you', but he knew Taduno would not approve.

Taduno put up his hands. 'We expect you to be a good neighbour,' he said, looking directly into the man's eyes.

The man looked away, but not before Taduno glimpsed the greed in his eyes.

'Oh yes, I'm a good neighbour.' The man's voice was weak.

Taduno realised at that moment that the man's heart was set on betraying them. TK was right: you can never appeal to the conscience of a greedy man, and you can never pay him enough. He turned to Aroli. 'TK was right,' he said simply.

Aroli nodded. 'So what do we do? We could still fall back on my plan.'

Taduno rejected Aroli's suggestion with a shake of his head. He must now attempt to stir the conscience of the man and his wife with his music. 'Come with me,' he said and rose to his feet. 'I want to make music in the street.'

Judah appeared at the door just then. 'You are here,' he said hesitantly, looking from Taduno to Aroli.

Taduno nodded at him with a smile. He wondered how the boy and Lela could be so different from their parents.

'I want to make music in the street,' he said to Judah and unslung his guitar. Then he walked calmly out into the street.

They all followed him.

*

He found a bench in the street. He knew he had to sit down to play the kind of music he wanted to play. So he sat down on the bench. Lela's mother joined them in the street with a look of horror on her face, sensing that trouble was on their doorstep. She sat on the pavement and folded her arms across her breasts. And as the first chords echoed from Taduno's guitar, her conscience began to torment her.

Slowly, his music spread throughout the neighbourhood, soft and colourful. The people began to gather one by one, cautiously, knowing soldiers were nearby. They remembered that the President had proscribed all association through music, but they were enthralled by the melodies that suddenly filled the empty spaces of their lives. So they came.

Among those gathered were Vulcaniser and several others from his street, who had not ventured out of their homes in days. They all came out to listen. And as they did, they shook their heads in wonder and joy.

Judah placed his palms on his little cheeks and stared at Taduno in astonishment. He thought: How could my parents ever think of giving such a wonderful man away?

*

Taduno told simple stories with his music, shifting from one story to the next with glorious ease. He spoke in the tone of a folksinger through his guitar to the large crowd that had gathered, and they understood the meaning of his music, the flow of his emotions.

He did not chastise Lela's parents with his music. Instead, he attempted to stir the conscience of all. And so he played beautiful wordless songs that his listeners would remember for a long time to come.

The soldiers soon showed up, causing many to take to their heels. They came with guns and tear gas and grenades, but Taduno's music softened their hearts and they lowered their guns and opened their mouths in amazement. Those who had taken off came back when they saw that the soldiers were not attempting to arrest anyone.

Momentarily transformed by the music they were hearing, the soldiers took off their helmets. They wiped soot from their faces with their bare hands. They wanted the people to see them as human beings, not monsters. But it was nothing more than a fleeting transformation. Soon, it occurred to them that in the end they had to answer to the President, not to the people, and certainly not to some musician, however brilliant he was. And so, they pushed through the crowd and arrested Taduno.

FOURTEEN

Because of the gravity of his offence – making music in public at a time when all association through music had been banned – they held him in solitary confinement in an underground cell that sunlight could never penetrate. The cell had a single weak bulb which his captors turned on from the corridor each time they came to see him. They were all afraid of his guitar and refused to touch it or take it away from him. And all the time they could hear him playing soft music that threatened to melt their hard souls.

He slept on the cold bare floor, and refused to touch the food they offered him on dirty flat plates. He claimed he was fasting, and they wondered why anyone would fast.

'Do you want to die?' a soldier asked him.

'No, I don't want to die, I want to live,' he replied.

'Why then are you fasting if you want to live?' the soldier asked.

'Because I need strength to go through my ordeal,' Taduno replied calmly.

The soldier could not believe his ears. He laughed at him as if he was a lunatic.

'You need food to give you strength,' the soldier said.

'No, I need to fast to get strength.'

'You'll starve to death if you don't eat.'

'I'll die if I eat. Food is not what I need now.'

'Well, suit yourself,' the soldier said, with a shrug. 'Go ahead and kill yourself if you want.'

Taduno gave him a kind smile.

*

He wondered if Lela was being held in conditions similar to his, and he shuddered at the thought. He imagined her, a fragile beauty, lying on a bare floor in an underground cell somewhere in the city. He imagined her, alone in darkness for hours, with no one to talk to except the soldiers who brought her food and water. He imagined her . . . And then realising that such thoughts would only intensify the nightmare of his incarceration, he banished them from his mind.

He refused to think about TK, Aroli, Judah, Vulcaniser and the rest of his neighbours, knowing that it would only sap his strength without changing anything. It gave him some comfort that Aroli would look after TK. So he looked inward and simply allowed music to flow from his heart.

In spite of themselves, the soldiers began to gather at the door of his cell to listen. And as they listened they began to perceive their own foul odour. They began to see their own faces, as in a mirror; the faces of the servants of an evil tyrant.

They saw how dirty their uniforms were. They saw the hopelessness that was their lot and that of their children and grandchildren and great-grandchildren. They began to understand that the reason they wore torn boots and smelly uniforms was because their master wanted their lives to remain in tatters. And they began to understand, too, that these tatters supported the prosperity of their master.

They began to sway to his music. They began to nod to his music. But they were too afraid to dance, knowing their master had eyes everywhere, and that soldiers were not supposed to dance.

*

On the morning of his fourth day in captivity, he asked for water. Because he had not taken water or food for three whole days, a soldier brought him water in a bucket.

'Drink water, please,' the soldier said. 'Drink for all the days that you have not drunk. Drink for all the days to come. We don't want you to die on us.'

'Thank you,' Taduno said.

He scooped water from the bucket with a plastic cup and he drank sparingly.

'Drink more, please,' the soldier begged. 'I can get you many more buckets of water if you want. There is food too. You can have any amount you want.'

'Thank you,' Taduno replied.

'Why are you thanking me?' the soldier asked. 'Are you thanking me because you want me to bring you food or because you want me to bring you more water?'

'I'm thanking you because you are very kind.'

'What about the food? Do you want it?'

'No, thank you. I don't want food. Thank you indeed.'

'Do you want more water? Do you want more of anything?'

Taduno shook his head. 'I have had enough water already. You can take the bucket away. I don't want more of anything.'

The soldier looked baffled. He could not understand what manner of man he was. Why would any man undertake a suicide mission? 'Well,' he muttered to himself and took the bucket of water away.

*

On the fifth day they allowed him to use a bathroom. They brought him a toothbrush and toothpaste in a plastic cup. They gave him a shaving stick too. And when he had taken his bath with a bucket of water, they brought him fresh clothes, a shirt and trousers – which were his perfect size – and a pair of shoes.

He refused to accept the shoes, insisting on wearing his own. They said it was okay with them if he wanted to wear his own shoes. But they insisted that he must have something to eat. So they brought him rice and a piece of chicken and a bottle of water. They set him a proper table in a bigger cell with a window open to bright sunlight.

Keeping his guitar on the table where he could see it, he ate slowly.

When he finished eating, he sat back to wonder why they were treating him so nicely. Why did they allow him to use a bathroom? Why did they bring him fresh clothes? As he asked himself these questions, he realised that he was about to be taken before someone very important.

*

He waited for several more days, in the bigger cell that enjoyed bright sunlight. The days dragged. The nights were even longer. He slept on a small wooden bed, with his guitar next to him. Anxiety ate at him. And he knew that this delay was a deliberate attempt to weaken him.

They brought him food and water every few hours, insisting that he must eat and drink. He obeyed them because he was at their mercy. He was too tense to play his guitar while he waited. He prayed he wouldn't have to wait for too long.

'What is happening?' he asked one of the soldiers.

'You are going to appear before our master,' the soldier replied.

'Who?'

'Mr President himself,' the soldier replied.

He swallowed and tried not to show his surprise. 'When?'

'Soon.'

'How soon is soon?'

'I don't know. We are waiting for instructions.'

He sighed and went to sleep.

He tried to sleep as much as possible to keep his mind from the waiting. But he couldn't sleep for too long at a stretch because they kept coming to wake him up, to offer him more food and water.

And they kept telling him they did not know how long he had to wait.

'Mr President is a very busy man, you see,' they would say to him.

FIFTEEN

They brought him before the President on a Sunday morning. He had lost count of the days, but they told him it was a Sunday. They said the President sees troublesome prisoners only on Sundays, and decides their fate on Mondays. If the prisoner is lucky he gets a reprieve on Tuesday. If he is not, he goes to the gulag on Wednesday.

'Your fate is no longer in your own hands,' a soldier told him, as they drove him to the President's office. 'In fact, your fate is no longer in the hands of man. It is now in the hands of a mighty man. All you can do now is pray.'

Taduno nodded and said: 'Thank you.'

'I said you should pray, I didn't say you should say thank you.'

'Thank you,' he repeated.

The soldier sighed. The fate of this prisoner is already sealed, he thought to himself.

*

He had more waiting to do when they got to the President's office. After a long chain of rigorous security checks and counterchecks, they brought him into a sprawling, tastefully furnished room. A handful of men dressed in flowing gowns sat on comfortable leather settees at one end of the room. He sat at the other end, with a single soldier by his side; and he could tell that he was the only prisoner in that room. All the others were potbellied VIPs.

He sighed and caressed his guitar.

*

He waited and waited.

The soldier guarding him warned him not to play his guitar when he was before the President.

'Why?' he asked innocently. 'Music is good.'

'Mr President does not like music,' the soldier said quietly. 'Music has caused too much trouble for his government.'

'I see,' he replied.

They fell silent again.

An hour or so later, the soldier began to snore quietly. Taduno turned to watch him sleep for a moment. Then he shook his head in pity, knowing the poor guy was exhausted.

He continued to caress his guitar, resisting the strong urge to play his music to the VIPs. None of them paid him any attention. They just kept whispering nervously amongst themselves, strategising ahead of their meeting with the President. He wondered if they were powerful politicians, or businessmen, or both. Judging by their potbellies and the smell of money about them, he assumed they must be both.

He waited for hours before he was ushered in to see the President, ahead of the potbellied men who had been waiting for much longer. The men looked at him as they took him in, wondering who he was and why he carried the guitar that seemed so disturbingly alive.

*

A female secretary showed him into the President's office and retreated silently, closing the sturdy door after her. At first, he felt lost in the vast office, and he wasn't sure whether to walk towards the huge mahogany desk at the far end of the room where a man was seated, or whether to remain still until he was summoned. He became even more confused when it occurred to him that he was alone with the man at the far desk whose face was buried in a thick file.

Summoning courage, he began to walk slowly towards the mahogany desk, towards the man who had not even bothered to look up to acknowledge his presence. Halfway to the desk, he stopped, realising that the man behind the desk was Mr President indeed. And he made up his mind to wait until he was summoned before proceeding any further.

He waited like that, in one spot, for almost an hour, while the President went through the file before him slowly and quietly. Finally, he pushed the file away and rose to his feet.

'Aha!' he said expansively. 'Please come over. So sorry to have kept you waiting.'

Taduno was disarmed by the President's effusive manner. He blinked a couple of times, then shuffled the remaining distance to the President's desk.

They shook hands. The President kept smiling broadly, that charming gap-toothed smile he always wore whenever he addressed the nation on TV. Taduno could not believe he was standing before the dictator who had ruled his country with an iron fist for eight years. He had always believed that the President's charming smile was purely for the camera. But standing before the man, he realised that he was very charming indeed.

He felt his head spinning.

'Very good to see you,' the President said to him, like an old friend. 'Please take a seat.' He appeared to be unperturbed about the guitar.

He waited for the President to sit down before pulling back a chair to sit down. And then, very carefully, he placed his guitar on the desk, between them, as if it was a witness to all that would follow.

'Nice guitar,' the President commented.

'Thank you.' He wanted to play his guitar, but he remembered the soldier's warning.

'Thank you for honouring my invitation,' the President began, 'especially on a Sunday like this.'

Invitation indeed! Taduno thought to himself. Aloud he said: 'It's a very great privilege.'

'I hope you have been very well treated by my men?' the President asked. The charming smile remained on his face. 'I hope they have catered for your every need?'

Taduno nodded. He did not want to say anything bad about the President's men. 'Oh yes, they have been excellent.'

'Very good!' the President nodded. 'I have an important meeting to attend now. You may leave, and I hope you will be kind enough to come back in a few days.'

Taduno was speechless. Before he knew it, a burly soldier came in to show him out.

At the door, he threw one last look back. The President's head was again buried in the thick file on his desk.

SIXTEEN

They took him back to solitary confinement in the underground cell which sunlight could never penetrate. And they left him there alone with his guitar in the dark.

The soldiers who looked after him were baffled. They could not understand why his case was so complicated. Who is this strange man? Why is his case so different from others? They asked him these questions, but the only answer they got was the beautiful sound of his guitar.

His music made the darkness of his cell bearable, fascinating even. He had never made music in solitary confinement before, and he discovered that the music he made was rich and colourful. He discovered that there was light in his music. Before then, he never knew there could be light in music. And now that he had discovered this amazing secret, he played his guitar more often.

*

Each time he played, he taught his captors a few things. He taught them that the quality of life you live is not necessarily measured by the amount of comfort you enjoy. He taught them that a life lived with honour and courage in a dungeon is more fruitful than one lived in denial in an ivory tower. He taught them that a beautiful smile is worth more than a powdered face. And he taught them to always look inward rather than outward.

He slept with contentment on the cold floor of his cell. He loved the solitude of the place; it afforded him the opportunity to compose his music in peace. He noted the faint echo that rose from the floor and stayed just below the sound of his music. He understood that his music superseded that faint echo. And he realised that as long as it stayed that way, they could never break him.

His captors began to love him more than they hated him. They knew that they hated him only because it was their duty to hate him, not because they really did. And they admitted to themselves that they loved him because he was such an easy man to love.

*

'Who are you?' one soldier asked in wonder after listening to him play for hours. 'Are you man or angel?'

He laughed quietly. 'I'm both,' he said. 'I'm man because I live in a cold solitary cell. I'm an angel because I live above my circumstances.'

The soldier shook his head in amazement. Those were the most profound words he had ever heard. He wished he could swap places with Taduno. He wished he could sleep on his cold bare floor and enjoy the peace he enjoyed on that floor. He wished he could become a prisoner and own a guitar no one could ever take from him.

*

A few days turned into many days and weeks. And all that while, except for when they turned on the weak bulb when they brought him food, the only light he had had was the light made by his music. His music turned what would have been pitch darkness into golden brightness.

He fasted on some days, and on others he ate and drank water sparingly. His captors came to respect his wish whenever he declined food and water. In fact, many of them wished they could go whole days without food and water, just like him.

At first, they compared his smile to that of the President in his ivory tower. But they soon realised that the President's smile did not, could never, have the enduring quality of the prisoner's smile. Realising that his smile was a great part of his essence, his captors began to smile too, hoping that their smiles would help them transcend their circumstances.

*

Taduno woke up one morning to discover that he had a neighbour in the adjoining cell which had been empty all along. He wondered who the other prisoner was.

Later, he caught a glimpse of the writer who made Kongi a household name, as they took him away after a few hours of solitary confinement. He caught a glimpse of his intellectual beard and proud gait, and he wondered what he had written this time. In tribute to the man, he played rousing songs on his guitar for hours.

'They brought Kongi here today,' one of his captors told him after he finished his songs.

'You mean the man who created Kongi?'

'We all know him as Kongi.'

'I see.'

'I wonder why they keep bringing him here. His eyes!' The soldier shook his head in disbelief.

'What about his eyes?'

'They are so penetrating they make us squirm in our boots.' He seemed to squirm even as he spoke the words.

'Maybe it is the purity in his eyes.'

'Does purity make people squirm?' the soldier asked.

He wanted to say, 'Purity makes unclean people squirm.' Instead he said, 'Maybe.'

'It terrifies me sometimes. His beard is so commanding. His hair, I cannot describe it.'

'Why did they bring him here?' he asked casually.

'It is about something he wrote again. He's always writing something, that man!'

'Yes, that man!' Taduno smiled. Very few men like him, he thought to himself.

He dreamed of the illuminated pages of books that night. The next day, a Sunday, they took him back to see the President.

SEVENTEEN

The President was nicer than the last time, and he did not keep him standing in the middle of his office for an hour. He attended to him straight away. He came round his desk eagerly to pull out a seat for him.

'How are you doing?' the President asked, with a warm smile, when they were comfortably seated with the guitar between them on the desk. 'I hope my men have looked after you very well?'

He returned the dictator's smile. 'Oh yes, they've been wonderful to me.'

For a brief moment he thought he saw the smile slip from the President's face.

'I am glad to hear that,' the President responded, eyeing the guitar slyly. He picked up a paper knife and began to tap an ugly sound on his desk, as if to say, 'You are not the only one who can make music. See, I can make music too!'

And then it suddenly dawned on Taduno. The President

wanted to break him down before beginning the interrogation, but he was unhappy that he had not succeeded so far.

'Why are you nodding your head and smiling?' the President asked suspiciously.

Taduno thought it was time to attempt to mess up the dictator's head too. 'I nod my head because it is my head,' he said. 'And I smile because it is good for me and I have the right to smile.'

'You have the right to smile?' the President smiled.

'Yes, I have the right to smile, even in my underground cell. I can smile anywhere, see?'

'I see,' the President nodded. 'Like you are smiling now.'

'Oh yes, like I'm smiling now. Smiling is good, see?'

The President nodded. 'I agree with you. Smiling is good. That is why I always smile so broadly when I address the nation. Smiling disarms your enemies.'

'I agree,' Taduno nodded. 'The nation is your enemy. So you disarm them.'

The President laughed. 'You are a very wise and brave man. But your braveness is greater than your wisdom.'

'Thank you.' He laughed too. 'But I think my wisdom is equal to my braveness.'

They studied each other for a few moments, two smiling warriors, unsure how to make the next attack.

'What is your name again?' the President asked suddenly.

'Taduno,' he replied.

'Taduno,' the President repeated, keeping his eyes on the guitar on the desk between them. 'Taduno.'

'Yes, Taduno. Just Taduno, no first or last name.'

'Do you know me? I mean, do you know what I am capable of, what I can do to you?'

Taduno shrugged. 'I don't know, and I don't care.'

He knew he was making a mistake even as he spoke those words. But he was determined not to allow the dictator to win this battle of the mind.

*

They took him to an underground cell beneath the one where they had previously kept him. And they left him there, with a lone soldier who sat in the corridor to cater for his needs.

He pushed his face into the cold bars of his cell gate. 'Why must they punish you by punishing me?' he said, out of pity for the poor soldier.

'They are not punishing me, they are punishing you,' the soldier replied.

'But you are sharing this grave, this underground space with me.'

'No, I'm not sharing it with you. I'm in the corridor, you are in the cell. I'm guarding you.'

'Guarding me against what?'

The soldier hesitated, unsure how to answer his question. 'Guarding you,' he said with a shrug.

'Are you guarding me against myself or against you? What are you guarding me against?'

'I don't know,' the soldier admitted. 'All I know is that you are being punished, and my duty is to ensure you undergo your punishment.'

'But your punishment is worse than mine.'

'What do you mean?'

'We are sharing this grave together. And you are carrying a burden, the burden of guarding me in this grave. I carry no burden. I'm free, but you are not. I'm free in this grave.'

'You are not free, and that's why I'm guarding you. Attempt to escape if you think you are free.'

'Free men don't escape. I'm free, so I do not need to escape. It is you who needs to escape. Try and leave this grave if you can.'

The soldier fell into silence. He looked down at the gun in his lap, and he realised how useless it was against his strange prisoner.

*

Sensing that his guard had descended into self-pity, Taduno tried to cheer him up. And as his music filled that cell under a cell, the darkness of the place gradually gave way to illumination, and he saw a smile on the face of his guard.

They enjoyed the music together for a long time; he playing, his guard listening. And in that place and time, they both felt free and lonely. But they bonded in their loneliness so that they began to see each other as friends; and as friends, they knew they had to look out for each other. And so they became safe in the knowledge that they had each other, which wasn't the result the dictator wanted to achieve.

'You are the first person to be sent down here in a long

time,' his guard said. 'In fact, only the second person ever to be sent down this deep.'

'I see,' he replied curiously. 'And who was the first?'

'The first was Kongi. He was a strange man. His hair and beard illuminated the place so much I felt dizzy with light.'

'That's what happens when you have a close encounter with the man. He illuminates you with light.'

'I agree with you,' the guard nodded.

A long silence followed.

'This is such a terrible place to be,' the guard said suddenly, with sadness in his voice. 'I wish I could get out.'

'Why do you stay here?'

He hesitated. 'Because I cannot get out. You are right, I cannot get out. I'm more of a prisoner than you. You are right.' He shook his head.

He did not know the right words to say to his guard. He picked up his guitar, and his fingers glided across the strings in a slow trance.

The guard listened.

*

His friendship with the guard developed, and each realised that all he had in that cold cell buried beneath a cell was the other. Sometimes the guard told him about his family: a wife and three young children; and of their futile struggle to survive in a city that was so expensive. At such times, Taduno lessened the guard's burden with the soft music of his guitar.

Convinced that the guard's friendship was genuine, he opened up to him about Lela. 'At first they said it was an arrest, then I discovered that she was actually kidnapped by the government.'

'Oh, that woman who is being held in custody by the President? She is your girlfriend?' the guard asked in surprise.

'Yes, she is. You know her?'

'I know her. We all know her,' the guard replied, with a wondrous shake of his head. 'She is a brave woman. No amount of interrogation has been able to break her. We have never come across a woman like her. She refused to give your identity away.' The guard paused and then asked with a frown, 'Why did they arrest you? I'm sure she wouldn't have given you away.'

'I was arrested not because she gave me away, but because I was making music in public against the President's order.'

'Your music is beautiful,' the guard said. 'We need your kind of music in our sad society.'

'Unfortunately, the President does not think so.'

'Have you told him you are the woman's boyfriend? He should let her go now that he has you. She is an innocent woman.'

Taduno remembered Sergeant Bello's words: 'Government does not believe in innocence,' he had said. He wondered how he was coping with work now that he had joined his voice to the murmuring of the people.

'No, I haven't told him. I have not had the opportunity to tell him. Moreover, if I were to tell him he wouldn't believe me. You see, my voice is my identity, but I lost it

135

and right now it is a croak. I must discover my voice to convince him I am the man he is looking for.'

'It all sounds so complicated and strange,' the guard said, shaking his head. 'Whatever, I respect you for your music. A man who plays such beautiful music cannot be a bad man. I'm sure the President will realise this in the end and release you and your girl.'

They lingered in silence for a while.

'I feel so sorry for her,' the guard spoke with sadness in his voice. 'She's being held in terrible conditions. Yet she is so brave.'

Taduno fought back his tears. He played his guitar. His music was soulful; it told the story of true love that can never be suppressed. The music travelled out of, and far beyond, that cell under a cell, and he prayed it would reach Lela wherever she was being held.

EIGHTEEN

He was shocked the morning the President came to visit him in his cell. He came alone, no bodyguard, and dismissed the lone soldier who had been on duty for weeks.

'Go home to your family,' the President said curtly to the soldier. 'Take some time off, but make sure you come back.' The dictator looked somewhat disturbed, but he still had the charming smile on his face.

The soldier saluted smartly and left, delighted at the opportunity to escape, but sad to be leaving Taduno behind. Their friendship had blossomed in the time they had stayed together. But because the President was watching, they could not exchange proper goodbyes.

The smile slipped off the President's face after the soldier had left, and he stared hard at Taduno who stared back hard at him. Slowly, they began to move round each other in a crouch, gauging each other, waiting for an opening.

It was the President who made the first move, a reckless

move warranted by the boldness he saw in the eyes of his adversary. And that move sparked off a fierce exchange.

'You and your type have tormented me with music for so long. But now you are at my mercy.' The President hissed.

'I still have my music, even in this underground cell,' Taduno responded, brandishing his guitar in the President's face. 'I still have my music. Even here, I can torment you with my music.'

'No!' the President screamed. 'No. We can end it here and now. I can bury you in this underground cell and no one will miss you.' His eyes were those of a man rattled by a strong opponent.

'You deceive yourself.' Taduno laughed mockingly. 'You deceive yourself.'

They continued to move round each other in a slow circle. Their feet made no sound in that cold cell; only the sound of their breathing could be heard. Each time the President attempted to close in, Taduno waved his guitar in his face, causing him to step back quickly.

'Do you know what I can do to you?' the President asked, breathing unevenly.

'Do you know what I can do to you with my music?' he responded. 'Do you know what I can do to you with this guitar?'

'I can get my men to take your guitar away from you.'

'No, you cannot. They are afraid of my guitar, the same way you are afraid of it.'

'I am not afraid of your guitar.'

'If you are not, try and take it away from me,' he taunted. 'Go on, take it away from me.'

The President broke out in a cold sweat. Taduno smiled in triumph. Drained of a great amount of energy, they stopped their slow circular movement and straightened up. And they stood there facing each other, panting for breath.

Realising he was up against a worthy opponent, the President raised his voice and called out to his men. Four soldiers came into the cell promptly, as if they had been waiting for their master's call all along.

'Get two seats!' the President ordered. The charming smile had returned to his face. He must not let his men see him otherwise.

*

They brought two chairs.

The dictator dropped into one. 'Sit down,' he said, nodding to the other chair opposite him.

Taduno obeyed.

The soldiers stood to attention behind the President.

'Now, let's get this straight,' the President began, as if no hostility had transpired between them earlier, 'you said your name is Taduno.'

'Yes,' he nodded.

'I understand you were caught making music in public against my order.'

'Yes.'

'Why did you disobey my order?'

'Because I believe your order was unjustified.'

'You believe my order was unjustified?'

'Yes. It violates my right to make public music.'

'You do not have rights. No one in this country has rights. This is not a civilian regime, this is a military regime, see?' The President smiled triumphantly.

'Well, I want my rights. Every citizen of this country wants their rights.'

The President shook his head in astonishment, unable to understand why anybody wanted rights under a military regime. He laughed in amusement.

Taduno remained quiet.

'Have you undertaken a search of his house?' the President asked, turning to his men.

'Not yet,' the most senior of the soldiers answered. 'We are waiting for instructions.'

'Go and conduct a thorough search of his house and report your findings back to me immediately. I want all the evidence you can find against this man.' To Taduno, he said: 'We are going to end this here and now. We will wait here for my men to come back.'

The soldiers saluted and left.

*

Not a single word passed between them while they waited for the soldiers to return. They sat in silence for hours. And each wondered how it was all going to end.

Eventually the soldiers returned. Terror gripped Taduno as he watched them drag Judah into the cell and dump him unceremoniously on the floor.

'What has the boy got to do with this?' he cried, jumping to his feet.

A soldier shoved him back into his seat.

'Uncle Taduno,' was all the boy could say. He looked cold and frightened.

'We found him in his house, sir,' the most senior soldier announced.

'What?' the President sounded baffled. 'I ask for evidence, you bring me a mere child? What has he got to do with anything?'

'We searched the house with a toothpick. That's the only evidence we found. We found him in the living room, sitting comfortably with his feet on a stool, as if he was waiting for us. So we brought him in.'

Taduno was stunned.

'Son, what's your name?' the President smiled at Judah.

Judah exchanged looks with Taduno, who nodded.

'My name is Judah,' the boy replied. To Taduno, he said: 'Don't worry, Uncle Taduno. TK is safe.'

For several moments the cell became a tomb of silence. And then the silence was broken by a single word, a question, whispered by the President.

'TK?'

'Leave the boy out of this.' Taduno's voice was flat.

'TK, the music producer? The same man my government is trying to find?'

'Yes, he was in my house,' Taduno replied. For Judah's sake, he made up his mind to tell the whole truth.

'And where is he now?'

'I don't know. I left him in my house before I was arrested.'

'And you said you checked the entire house?' The President turned to his soldiers.

'Yes, sir.'

'Including the attic?' Taduno added inquisitively.

'Yes, including the attic. We checked everywhere.'

The President cleared his throat. 'Just so we get this absolutely straight. Who exactly are you? What is TK to you?'

Taduno took a deep breath. 'My name is Taduno, the musician you all forgot.'

'What do you mean?'

Taduno explained as best he could.

'Wait a minute,' the President interrupted, 'are you saying you are the great musician my government is looking for? The one whose name and face we have all forgotten? The one whose girlfriend is in our custody?'

'That's exactly what I'm saying.'

'Well, there is only one way to find out. Your voice is your identity. So sing a song, prove you are who you say you are.'

'I've lost my voice. I received one beating too many from your men, and that affected my vocal cords. TK's trying to help me discover my voice, that's why I brought him to stay in my house.'

'So you are saying you don't have the magic voice of the musician we are looking for?'

'Yes.'

'Then how do I know you are the man we are looking for? How do I know you are not a fake?'

'I could play you my guitar. Maybe that would help you make up your mind. Or you could bring Lela to identify me. She'll remember me.'

For a few moments, the President tapped one foot on the floor in deep thought. He was not prepared to give him the advantage of playing his music. 'Go and get the girl,' he said, turning to the soldiers behind him.

*

Thirty minutes later, they dragged Lela in, struggling and sobbing. Her hair looked wild and unkempt and she was thin as a broomstick.

Taduno jumped to his feet.

Judah rushed towards his sister. '*Anti* Lela!' he shouted. A soldier held him back. He struggled in vain to break away from the soldier's grip. Huge tears rolled down his face. '*Anti* Lela!' he cried out again.

Slowly, Lela adjusted to her environment. She saw Judah. She saw Taduno. But all the other men in the room appeared as blurry images to her. She closed her eyes in disbelief. When she opened them, Judah and Taduno were still there. She saw them quite clearly. And then she crumbled to the floor.

Taduno rushed to her, with his guitar dangling from his shoulder. One or two soldiers attempted to hold him back, but the President's voice stopped them like a cold whip. 'Don't touch him!'

He went down on his knees and folded Lela carefully into his arms. They stared at each other in disbelief. He closed his eyes in gratitude. This was the moment he had so desperately longed for.

'Taduno?' Lela whispered.

He was too overjoyed to speak. He held her even tighter. They wept quietly with joy.

Judah's small voice shattered the silence and all that remained of the mystery that had swallowed his identity. 'I remember you now, Uncle Taduno!' the boy said wondrously. 'Yes, I remember you now!'

And then, one by one, the other men began to remember him. The President shook his head as he remembered, wondering how they could all have forgotten.

*

Taduno and Lela clung to each other, rocking silently. At last Taduno leaned back to look into her eyes. They both laughed, like two little kids hiding a beautiful secret from the world. Again they hugged, then they kissed briefly, giggling as one. In that time and place, they became oblivious of the world around them. Nothing mattered any more, except that they were together at last.

The President and his soldiers were gripped by the unfolding drama.

Judah was speechless.

'You haven't been eating well,' Lela complained, pulling back to study Taduno's face. 'Why?' she asked with a pout.

'I haven't been eating well because I missed you so much. Look at you,' he laughed. 'You look so beautiful despite all you have been through.'

'You must eat well, please,' she warned him gently.

'From now on I will.'

Looking into each other's eyes, the impulse to talk about

Lela's letters overcame them simultaneously, but each realised how dangerous it could be. They realised that if the President knew about the letters, an inquest would follow and the punishment would be swift and far-reaching. So they just looked into each other's eyes and nodded in quiet understanding. They giggled some more, happy that they could exchange secrets even with the dictator watching.

Their love was infectious. A morbid joy coursed through the President as he realised that it was the force of that very love that he would use to break them and get Taduno to do his bidding.

'Come, Judah!' Lela cried happily, beckoning to her brother.

The boy rushed over and spread his little arms around his sister and Taduno. They looked like one big happy family held together by the fragility and innocence of a little boy.

The President smiled. Now he knew the weakness of his formidable adversary. He smiled some more with a slow nod of his head. He had seen enough. Now he was ready to make the next move.

*

The President gave rapid orders to his soldiers, and they stepped forward and tore the lovers and the boy apart with brute force. And as they dragged Lela out of the cell, her wretched cries joined those of Taduno and Judah, reverberating throughout that underground world and shaking the foundations of all things.

After they had taken Lela away, Taduno and Judah continued to cry, the loudness of their cry embracing the echo of Lela's.

Shouting angry orders, the soldiers finally managed to quieten them and that tomb world regained its deathly silence. The President rubbed his hands together. He and Taduno must finish it there and then in that cold cell, now that a great mystery had been unravelled. And so, in one deft move, he put his chips on the table. Not with the recklessness known to most gamblers, but with the caution of a man who wanted to win at all costs.

'Your girlfriend remains my prisoner until you use your music to promote my government,' the President said. He rose to his feet and began to pace the cell.

'I'll praise your government with my music. But you must let Lela go first.'

'No, she remains my prisoner. I will let you and the boy go, but she remains my prisoner. And you must hand TK over.' The President brought the boy cleverly into the bargain, conceding him at the same time to make it difficult for his adversary to press for more.

Realising he was losing ground, Taduno fought back doggedly. 'I cannot praise your government with my music until I discover my voice again. I need TK to do that. I also need him to produce the music. You cannot touch him. And you must withdraw all the soldiers from the streets. Their presence creates fear and tension in society, and I cannot make music that way.'

'Fine, I will not touch TK. I will instruct my men to let him be. I will withdraw my men from the streets. But the girl remains my prisoner.' The President's voice had a cold finality that sent a chill up Taduno's spine.

'Wait!' Taduno cried as the President turned to leave the cell. 'Wait! Please release Lela, and I promise I will praise your government with my music. I promise. I will do anything you want, but please release her.'

The charming smile returned to the President's face, seeing that he had an advantage over his stubborn adversary once again. He could sense victory not too far away now. He thrust his decisive blow.

'You have four weeks to prove your loyalty to my government with a hit song,' he spoke in a friendly tone. 'If you fail, you will never see your girl alive again. As I speak, you are a free man. You leave with the boy, I leave with the girl. When your assignment is done, both you and TK will be very richly rewarded.' He fired instructions at his men and walked briskly out of the cell.

NINETEEN

They drove him and Judah home in a stretch limousine that brought out the entire neighbourhood when it parked in front of his house. Judah came out first, amidst a gasp of surprise that rippled down the entire street. And then as Taduno stepped out, like an armoured knight, they all remembered him as suddenly as they forgot him.

They remembered him as the great musician who championed the cause of the people; the ingenious maker of simple music, whose songs adorned their hearts and gave them strength in the lopsided fight against the military.

Like a sudden ocean surge, they rushed towards him and lifted him high on their shoulders, chanting his name, glad that he had returned to their midst. They danced with him all over the neighbourhood, and soon, news of his arrival spread across the city.

Within hours, his street flooded with fans and well-wishers. And a huge party that would rock the entire city for two days began.

'I knew you were right all along,' Aroli said with uncontainable delight, when he finally had access to him. 'I knew we were the ones who forgot. Look, see how much they love you! How could we have forgotten?'

Taduno smiled at Aroli, and then at Judah who had not returned to his parents' house since their release that afternoon.

'Thank you for letting me stay in Uncle Taduno's house earlier,' Judah said to Aroli.

Aroli laughed. 'But you got arrested!'

'Yes, but I saw *Anti* Lela.' A hint of sadness crept into the boy's voice. 'If you had not allowed me to stay in Uncle Taduno's house the soldiers wouldn't have taken me to see her.'

Taduno turned to Aroli for an explanation.

Aroli explained that Judah had come to him that morning to ask if he could spend time in Taduno's house. Although a very odd request, he had let him in and went about his business only to return later and learn that soldiers had raided the house and taken the boy away.

'Thank God he wasn't detained,' Aroli concluded with a sigh of relief.

'Where is TK?' Taduno asked, his eyes fixed intently on Aroli.

'Don't worry about TK for now. He is safe,' Aroli replied evasively.

Before Taduno could say another word, he was swarmed by a new set of well-wishers who had just arrived.

*

Everyone wanted to hug and congratulate him on his triumphant return. And only the intervention of Vulcaniser, who had taken charge of his security, along with seven handpicked men, saved him from being smothered by the rapturous crowd.

Vulcaniser and his men prised him away from the crowd into the safety of his house where he immediately succumbed to sleep, exhausted from his tortuous encounter with the dictator. While the street rocked, and more and more people continued to arrive, Taduno slept deeply.

The sound of celebrating drums shook the entire city. On Channel 4 News a rare smile lit up the face of the newscaster as she spoke excitedly about the return of Taduno, the great musician the world forgot. 'The country has a hero again!' she said. 'The people have someone to look up to again. Freedom possibly beckons to us all!'

Listening to the newscaster in his office, the President nodded his satisfaction – Taduno was the right man to give his regime credibility. He often watched Channel 4 because it enabled him to gauge the mood of the country. He felt extremely pleased that very soon Taduno's voice would lead the people, but not in the way the newscaster imagined. She did not know what the President knew. She did not know that Taduno had sold out.

*

The party went on for two days, and Taduno slept all that while, snoring lightly, delighted that the world now remembered him. Aroli and Vulcaniser took turns to keep watch while he slept. In the street, the noise was joyful and ceaseless.

When he woke up the morning of the third day, everyone had returned to their homes. He remained still in bed for a few moments. Then, seeing Aroli sitting in a chair at one end of the room, he raised himself groggily on one arm and asked: 'Where is TK?'

'You are awake!' Aroli said eagerly. He jumped up from the chair where he had been reading a book and rushed to his bedside. 'How are you feeling?' he asked, ignoring Taduno's question.

Taduno ignored Aroli's question too. He sat on the bed with his feet on the floor. He surveyed the bedroom slowly. Then he asked again: 'Where is TK?'

Aroli knew that he could no longer evade his question. He pulled a chair close to the bed and sat down. 'TK had to escape when you were arrested. Vulcaniser and I helped him because we knew they would come to search your house sooner or later. And we knew they would kill him if they found him here.'

'Where did he go?' His voice was a fearful whisper.

'I don't know. We gave him a haircut so that it would be difficult for the soldiers to identify him, and then he left through the back door with his bag.'

'You cut off his Afro?'

'Yes, we did. It was for his own good.'

Taduno shook his head in dismay.

Vulcaniser walked into the bedroom then. 'You are awake,' he said happily. 'I hope you are well rested?'

151

'I need to find TK,' said Taduno. 'I need to find him if I'm to secure Lela's release.'

Vulcaniser wondered what TK had to do with Lela's release. He turned to Aroli with his eyebrows raised.

'He needs to find TK urgently. It is important,' Aroli explained.

'I will send my men into the streets to begin an immediate search,' Vulcaniser said, and hurried out of the room.

*

While Vulcaniser was away, Taduno briefed Aroli about his encounter with the President. He left out the details of his ordeal in the underground cells. But he told him that he had seen Lela, and how pitiable her condition was.

'You saw her?' Aroli's voice was tinged with fear.

'Yes.'

'Why didn't you get the President to release her since he now remembers you? After all, you are the one they are looking for, not Lela.'

'He insists I must praise his government with a hit song within four weeks. Lela is his bargaining chip. I explained that I need to discover my voice first, and that I need TK to do so. He agreed to call off the hunt for TK to allow him to work with me.'

They fell into a long silence.

Finally, Aroli spoke. 'The people are singing your praises, looking up to you. You are not going to crush their hopes by supporting the regime with your music now, are you?'

'I have no choice.' Taduno's voice was quiet.

'You have a choice.'

'What choice do I have? Allow Lela to die? All along, the plan was for me to discover my voice, praise the government with my music and secure her release.'

'Yes, that was what we agreed. But that was before we remembered you. Now that we remember you, the whole country is looking up to you. If you go ahead and support the regime with your music, our hopes will be crushed. The regime will have won. Tyranny will have won, and people will say that you were responsible for conceding that defeat. It will be remembered that you sold the people out.'

'I'm selling no one out!' Taduno exploded.

'That's the way it looks.'

Taduno jumped to his feet and stormed into the bathroom.

*

He emerged forty minutes later in a white bathrobe, refreshed but strained. Downstairs in the living room, he found Aroli in a distant mood.

'I guess there is nothing left to say,' Aroli said, rising from his seat. 'The way I see it, the priority is to find TK, and then you will have to discover your voice and make music to praise the government.'

Taduno did not respond.

Aroli shrugged. 'I'll go and see what progress Vulcaniser and his men are making and report back to you.' He went out and closed the door quietly after him.

For a while Taduno roamed his living room, unable to coordinate his thoughts. The only clear image in his mind was of Lela's face and the anguish she bore so helplessly. The image passed, replaced by that of TK, without his distinctive Afro cut.

Wondering how he would find TK, he went up to his bedroom and began to get dressed.

*

Taduno enjoyed smiles and greetings in the street just like the good old days. Everyone stared at his guitar in admiration; they wanted to know when he would rattle the dictator with another song. He had no answer for them, and he wept in his soul knowing he could no longer live up to their expectations.

He refused to look into people's eyes. He could not laugh with them or smile at them; his conscience forbade him. So he simply looked away and spoke to them from the corner of his mouth.

'We have not been able to find TK,' Vulcaniser updated him.

A small crowd of men gathered around him in front of Vulcaniser's workshop. Everyone patted him on the back and assured him that they would help him to find TK. Vulcaniser had told them how important it was, they said.

He nodded gratefully at them.

'I cannot thank you all enough,' he managed to say. 'I'll start a search for TK too, from tomorrow. I'm sure that together we will find him soon.'

They answered in chorus, nodding their heads eagerly.

Afterwards, they insisted on going for a meal with him at Mama Iyabo's restaurant. More people joined them as they made their way there, and, in the end, the restaurant was so packed many had to stand or sit on the bare floor. But they did not mind. They were in the company of a hero whose music would liberate them from the ruthless dictator.

*

'Where is Aroli?' Taduno asked Vulcaniser as they ate.

'He has not returned since he went out in the morning,' Vulcaniser replied. 'I'm sure he is still combing the streets for TK. He said we must find him urgently.'

'I wish he would understand.' Taduno spoke his thought aloud, a sad look on his face.

'Oh, I'm sure he does,' Vulcaniser said as he wiped his soup bowl clean with his last morsel of pounded yam.

Taduno nodded absentmindedly. Vulcaniser did not understand what he meant, and he did not intend to explain to him.

They finished eating, and all who could afford to contributed towards the bill. Then they begged him to play for them. He obliged, knowing that he would soon betray them irredeemably. He played a very slow tune that brought tears to his eyes. 'Tell me, what hope is there for the man who betrays his own people to save love?' he asked with his wordless song. But no one could console him with an answer.

155

*

Later, he went to see Judah at home.

He found him seated in the midst of his friends in his parents' compound, regaling them with fantastic stories of his encounter with the President which culminated in the limo ride back home.

'Uncle Taduno!' Judah cried, jumping to his feet.

'Lion of Judah!' he hailed.

'That's me!' Judah responded happily.

They embraced.

The other kids gathered around them, stretching to shake hands with Taduno.

He had assured Judah during the journey in the limo that he would secure Lela's release, and Judah had full confidence that he would keep his promise. But the boy did not know that it would be at the cost of betraying everyone who looked up to him and had faith in his music. The boy did not know that his sister had become the most prized asset to both Taduno and the President; the queen in a ruthless game of chess. The boy did not know. But it wouldn't have mattered even if he did. All he wanted was to have his beloved sister back. He could not care less what happened to the rest of the country.

'How are you?' Taduno asked, ruffling the boy's hair.

'I'm fine. And you?'

'I'm fine too.'

'I came to your house a few times, but Uncle Aroli and Vulcaniser told me you were sleeping.'

'Oh yes, I was. I have not slept well in weeks.'

Judah hesitated. 'My parents came to see you too, when you were sleeping.'

'Did they?'

'Yes, they did.'

'Are they home now?'

'Yes.'

'Let's go in. I want to see them.' To the rest of the kids, he said, 'Go and play football, Judah will join you soon.'

The kids screamed with delight and dispersed into the street in search of a football.

*

Lela's parents were too ashamed to look at Taduno when he walked into their living room with Judah. They greeted him in a stiff manner, not because he was not welcome in their home, but because they were embarrassed. Sensing their discomfort, Judah retreated quietly to his room.

'Judah told me you came to my house,' Taduno spoke cheerfully, when he had taken a seat.

The man simply nodded. His wife sighed.

He knew how they felt. He knew exactly how betrayers feel. In fact, he realised, he was worse than them now that he had agreed to betray an entire country.

'Please don't feel so bad for wanting to report TK's presence in my house to the authorities. Don't see it as betrayal, but as a duty imposed on you by law.' He wanted to purge his conscience.

Lela's parents felt a little relieved when he mentioned that very heavy word – betrayal.

'We are so sorry.' The man found his voice.

'Please forgive us,' his wife begged, wringing her hands and crying quietly. 'It was because we forgot everything about you. We did not even remember you as Lela's boyfriend. We wouldn't have dreamt of betraying you if we had not forgotten. You have always been so dear to us. Please forgive us.'

He felt ashamed that they could not see his own guilt. 'Please forgive me too,' he said. 'Forgive me even though you can't see my guilt.' He smiled hopefully at them.

They did not understand what he meant. But they smiled back at him all the same.

'Lela will be released soon,' he promised them. 'I have seen her. She's doing okay.'

'Judah told us,' the man said, his eyes alight with hope. 'He told us everything. How they brought him before the President. And how they brought Lela also. He told us you defied the soldiers to console her. Thank you so much.'

'Thank you, Taduno,' the wife whispered.

He hugged them when he stood up to go. Judah came out of his room to say goodbye.

'Your friends must be waiting to hear more stories,' he said to the boy, with a laugh.

Judah smiled.

Taduno left with sadness in his heart.

*

That afternoon, Baba *Ajo* led a delegation from his street to visit him. Among them was the pretty orange seller who called him Oga Musisan with a demure smile on her tired face and the bony thug who hailed Oga Musisan with his fists in the air. Taduno received them warmly. He offered them cold drinks and a bowl of fried chicken which he ordered from Mama Iyabo's restaurant.

They refused to eat or drink. Their hearts were too heavy for that. They had come to apologise for the rude reception they gave him the last time he visited their street. They had also come to express their shame at the way they treated TK. He could tell from their faces how sorry they were. And he smiled at them saying: 'We all make mistakes in life. That's why we are human beings.'

'Our mistakes are too grave for words,' Baba *Ajo* spoke slowly. 'We have come to beg for forgiveness. That's why I came with this delegation, so that you can hear from their mouths directly. Whatever you hear from them, they speak on behalf of everyone on our street.' A sigh escaped him.

'Oga Musisan, please forgive us,' the thug began, raising his fists in the air, before folding his arms across his chest. 'It was not so much our fault, it was because we forgot you. And how could we have forgotten you like that? Please forgive our madness. Forgive the madness that also made us treat TK so terribly. Ah! A man who did so much more than gofment can ever do for us. Baba *Ajo* warned us, but we would not listen. Ah! Our sins are too great to be forgiven.' He shook his head.

'And now we can't even find TK to beg his forgiveness!' the orange seller wailed. 'Will he ever find the heart to forgive us? Will he ever want to live amongst us again? Our lives can never be complete without him. Oga

Musisan, we beg you to help us beg TK when you find him.' The young woman began to cry.

Everyone that came took turns to speak, to express their deepest regrets. They all spoke very well, with their arms across their chests, unable to understand the madness that drove them to do all that they did, and to forget all that they forgot.

Baba *Ajo* gave the closing speech. 'It is too late to shed tears now. What's done is done. But our people say to sin is human and to forgive is divine. I will not deliver a long speech. Please accept our pleas and forgive us. When you find TK, please pass our messages to him.'

All said and done, they settled down to devour the bowl of fried chicken, and they washed it down with cold drinks. They ate with concentration, not sparing the bones. And they felt light and happy as they returned to their street.

*

It was close to midnight when Aroli came to knock on his door. He had roamed the city in search of TK for hours. Taduno was taken aback when he saw how beaten Aroli looked.

'Where have you been all day?' he asked, stepping back to let Aroli in and shutting the door quietly.

'I've been all over the city,' Aroli replied, dropping into a chair.

Taduno sat opposite him and leaned forward eagerly.

'There's no trace of TK anywhere,' Aroli said, staring at the floor. Taduno stared at the floor too.

TWENTY

Taduno discovered that the soldiers had been withdrawn from the streets as he travelled round the city the next day.

In the absence of soldiers, the streets became brighter and people went about their activities with primordial passion. The bus conductors resumed their sing-song and charmed commuters travelled longer distances, exploring parts of the city previously unknown to them.

Taduno's re-emergence aroused emotions everywhere he went. People begged to hear his music, and he complied, but only with his guitar. They wondered why he chose to remain silent. He tried to tell them, through his guitar, that he had sold his voice to the devil. He tried to tell them that the next time they heard his voice it would be in praise of the dictator who had oppressed them for so many years. He strummed his confessions, delicately, piti-fully. But he did not know whether they understood him. He did not know whether they listened to his confessions because they were too pained not to or because they were too enthralled with his music to stop listening. His music assumed a soulful new sound, plaintive to hear. Nothing remained of its sublime joy.

*

He travelled on long and small buses with the people he would soon betray. He mingled with them at rowdy bus stops, under the burning sun. He gave them stiff smiles, made small talk with them, and forced himself to laugh with them as he searched for TK, the man who must help him to save Lela.

Aroli begged to go with him, but he refused, not wanting to taint his friend with the impending atrocity.

'You have done enough for me,' he said to Aroli. 'I have to do the rest myself. I'm prepared to pay the price for love. You don't have to pay that price with me.'

'I have learned a thing or two from you,' Aroli said. 'Maybe I will learn to love like you one day.'

For a moment he dwelled on Aroli's words. And then he asked himself: What is the real meaning of love? When is love a crime? He knew the answer to his second question. Love is a crime when you love one person at the expense of the whole world. Of this crime he had become hopelessly guilty. He wondered if love would exonerate him in the end.

*

He attempted to sing with his half-baked voice as he went

round the city, but the sound that came out caused his listeners to cringe.

The Channel 4 newscaster told the country: 'Something isn't right about Taduno's voice. It lacks the passion that used to inspire joy in us. What is happening to him? What is happening to us?' She left the questions hanging, and then she added: 'We still love him dearly. We still want his voice to lead us. The whole nation is waiting.'

In his office the President smiled to himself, pleased with how things were going. A week had passed. Three more to go.

*

Every night, when the gentle breeze lifted at TBS, the homeless men gathered to listen to Taduno's music. Even though they knew something had changed about it, they were still enthralled. They were joyful that they now remembered him, like the rest of the world, and they wondered why they had forgotten him in the first place. The more they wondered, the more confused they became. And so they stopped wondering.

His music always paid tribute to their woes, and this endeared him to them. Sometimes he slept with them in the square, and his music made the cold nights more tolerable.

He loved to listen to their snoring in the quiet night. He loved the way they snored without worries. And when they slapped angrily at the mosquitoes, their snoring took a lull before picking up again in second gear.

The homeless man who gave him information about TK on his first night at the square was named Thaddeus. Before he became homeless, Thaddeus worked as an automobile engineer. He was doing well at his profession. And then he dreamed of building a made-in-Nigeria car, and made the mistake of going to the government with his dream. They were appalled and killed it because they wanted to continue to patronise car makers from Japan, the US, France and Germany. After they returned his dream to him in tatters, he woke up one day and found himself homeless. And so he began to live at the square.

He told Taduno his story on a quiet starlit night, while the others were snoring. They watched the stars together. Taduno marvelled at how beautiful they were. Thaddeus attempted to count them – in the same hopeful, futile way he had attempted to build a made-in-Nigeria car.

*

Thaddeus told him that he had not seen TK in many weeks. 'But I'm sure he will come back,' he reassured him.

'I hope he comes back soon,' said Taduno, sounding desperate.

'Why do you want him back so bad?'

'Because I need him to help me make good music again,' Taduno replied.

'I see,' Thaddeus said.

The square became quiet.

'It's a matter of life and death,' Taduno continued. 'Please tell the others to keep their eyes and ears open. If they see TK or hear anything about him they should let me know immediately.'

Thaddeus nodded. 'I will tell them. But if I may ask, why would making good music be a life-and-death thing? I don't know much about music-making, but I believe it should be a beautiful experience. Please excuse me if I'm wrong.'

'You are absolutely correct. Yes, you are. But making music has become a burden for me. It is not something I can explain.'

'Nothing is too complex to be explained.'

He digested Thaddeus' words for a moment, and he failed to understand how such an intelligent man could end up at the square. He wondered if he would end up like Thaddeus one day. The thought sent a chill up his spine.

'Yes,' he agreed, 'nothing is too complex to be explained. Maybe I should say it is not something I want to explain.'

'That sounds better. It is not everything that must be explained,' Thaddeus said and sighed.

'Did you ever make any attempt to revive your dream?' he asked, looking away from Thaddeus.

'I tried. It didn't work.'

The cold night bonded them. When they became silent, the snores in the square invaded their respective thoughts.

Taduno wondered at his new friend Thaddeus. And he wondered, especially, at himself. He picked up his guitar, and he strummed a tune that was barely audible in the silent night.

TWENTY-ONE

Finding it increasingly difficult to rehearse in his own house now, Taduno began to spend his nights at TBS. He would sit among the homeless men and play his guitar for many hours without singing. As they listened, his music stirred old memories.

He played patiently; they listened attentively. When he stopped, the snoring began. He would then retire to the far end of the square, away from everyone, and play his guitar with a softness that teased the night breeze. And he would sing quietly along.

Sometimes Thaddeus came to listen to him while the others slept.

'Your voice used to be much better than it is now,' Thaddeus commented on one occasion, during an interlude. 'What happened?'

'I had an accident and lost my voice,' he replied. 'I'm trying to discover it.'

'I'm so sorry to hear that,' Thaddeus said.

'Thank you.' He hesitated. 'Any word about TK?'

'Not yet. But I'm sure he will turn up eventually.'

'I hope so. I'm running out of time.'

'What's the hurry? Do you have a deadline to meet?'

Taduno hesitated. 'No, I haven't any deadline. It's just that I'm eager to make music again,' he replied and cringed at the half-truth of his words.

'Take it easy,' Thaddeus advised patiently. 'Nothing done in a hurry is ever done well. Take it easy.'

Taduno nodded. 'I agree with you, and I wish I could take your advice. Unfortunately, I cannot.'

Thaddeus rose to leave. 'Time to go to bed,' he said with a chuckle. 'Have a good rehearsal.'

'Thanks and good night.'

'Goodnight, my friend.'

Thaddeus raised his collar against the cold and left Taduno to join the competing snorers at the other end of the square.

*

While he played among the homeless men the following night, a string broke on his guitar for the first time in his career, forcing his music to end. For a few moments, a nervous silence descended upon the square. And then someone cleared his throat noisily, causing everyone to throw fearful looks around. The noisy throat clearer repeated his act a second time, a warning that he wanted to speak now that the sound of music was dead. Everyone waited for what he had to say. When he spoke, his words were simple and clear. 'When music is silent you hear the laughter of the tyrant,' he said.

Taduno digested the words slowly. He replayed the voice in his mind. Then, realising that it was the voice of Aroli, he shook his head in amazement.

'Aroli?' he called out.

'Yes, Taduno,' Aroli replied, standing up in the midst of the ragged men and making his way through them.

'What brings you here?'

'To see what progress you are making.'

Taduno managed a painful laugh. 'A string is broken on my guitar,' he said.

'So sorry about that,' Aroli said as he stopped before Taduno on the bench where he was seated.

'It is the first time.' He laughed uncertainly.

'There's always a first time.'

The other men remained silent. They had nothing to say. So they simply listened to the conversation between Taduno and Aroli.

'Welcome to the square,' Taduno said.

'It is beautiful out here.'

'Yes, it is,' Taduno said, rising to his feet.

'I just had to come. I wanted to see how you are getting on.'

'It's nice of you to come. Meet my new neighbours,' Taduno said with a laugh. Raising his voice, he said: 'Everyone, meet my dear friend, Aroli.'

'Hi!' the men said in unison.

'Hi!' Aroli said, raising his hand in greeting.

Taduno felt warmth he hadn't experienced in a long

time. He introduced Aroli to Thaddeus and the three of them chatted while the others retired to their various sleeping positions.

'Since my guitar is broken and I cannot rehearse tonight, I guess I'll have to go home,' Taduno said.

A chill descended on the square when he and Aroli left to catch the last bus home.

He spent all night mending the broken string of his guitar.

*

Vulcaniser paid him a visit in the morning wearing a very worried look.

'We've searched the city and there's no sign of TK,' he said. 'I believe he must have left the city.'

'He couldn't have left the city,' Taduno shook his head. 'He has nowhere else to go. His life is here. He must be somewhere out there. Look, I appreciate your effort. Leave it to me, I'll find him somehow.'

'I hope we have not disappointed you?' Vulcaniser said, lowering his head.

'Not at all! You have done very well. I appreciate all your efforts.'

Vulcaniser's face brightened. 'We will not stop looking. We will continue to keep our eyes and ears open. If TK is still in the city, somebody will see him or hear something about him eventually.'

Taduno nodded and thanked him once again.

They shook hands warmly.

After Vulcaniser had left, Taduno picked up his guitar, which he had successfully mended. For a while, he simply paced the living room holding the guitar in one hand. Then he played one of his old songs. Although the guitar was as good as it was before, the music refused to come together. He tried for several hours without success. And then, realising that his house was no longer a place where beautiful music could be made, his heart began to beat with fear.

*

Aroli was not there to share his fear; he was busy chasing one property deal or the other all over the city. So, feeling somewhat desolate, Taduno left for TBS earlier than usual that day. The place was teeming when he arrived there. For several hours he jostled among the crowd, acknowledging greetings here and there. And then he bumped into Thaddeus, who was panting as if he had just completed a marathon.

'Thank God you are here!' Thaddeus said, gasping for breath. He pulled Taduno away from the crowd.

'What's the matter?' Taduno asked anxiously.

'I saw TK. I called out to him but he disappeared into the crowd.'

'When did you see him?' His mouth was dry.

'About an hour ago. I have been searching through the crowd for him ever since, without luck.'

'Are you sure he is the one you saw?'

'Yes, I'm sure. Even though he has cut his Afro, I feel certain he is the one I saw.'

Taduno shook with excitement. He had not mentioned to Thaddeus that TK no longer wore his Afro.

'What did he look like without his Afro?' he asked.

'He looked forlorn. I cannot describe it – almost as if he was no longer of this world.'

'Why didn't you stop him?'

'I tried to get to him but my movement was hampered and he disappeared into the crowd. I believe he is running away from something.'

'He is a free man now. He doesn't have to run!' There was utter dejection in Taduno's voice.

Thaddeus looked lost. He wondered what Taduno meant, but not wanting to ask any questions, he said: 'Maybe he will sleep at the square tonight.'

'I hope he does. But in the meantime let's continue to search for him, please.' Taduno's voice was urgent.

They agreed to comb the crowd in opposite directions. And they went about it as swiftly as they could.

*

They got back together on an old bench that creaked under their weight. Their search had been fruitless.

Soon the homeless men started to converge. And then it was time for him to regale them with music.

'I don't feel like playing tonight,' he whispered to Thaddeus.

'You cannot let us down!' Thaddeus whispered back. 'We look forward to this every night. It is about the only thing we look forward to. It makes sleeping in this square bearable.'

He sighed. 'Okay, I'll try.'

So he played his guitar.

Because his mind wasn't settled, he finished earlier than usual. Then he went round with Thaddeus, staring at the faces of his audience one after the other. TK was not among them. They went round a second time, still without any luck.

'But I saw him,' Thaddeus said.

Taduno suppressed a sigh of frustration.

*

It was a strange night. Even though he rehearsed with the minimum volume, the sound of his music seemed to fill the square.

He was still playing way past midnight when a car pulled up in the darkness. He heard the screech of tyres. Soon, he could hear the sound of approaching footsteps, and he could tell that they were the footsteps of a very important man. He continued to play, unconcerned about who the approaching man could be. His music became louder, the sound of snoring dropped a notch – but they continued to combine well in the grand music that resonated in the square.

And then he heard a voice, and only then did he realise who was now standing before him.

'I see you are working hard to discover your voice.'

Taduno stopped playing and looked up in surprise at the President. He rose slowly to his feet and looked fearfully around.

'Don't worry, I came alone,' the President said.

'Alone?' Taduno repeated incredulously. 'You venture out at this time of night alone?'

'Why not? After all, I'm a General. I have fought many wars and I have tasted countless victories. Why should I be afraid to explore my own territory?'

Taduno swallowed. 'Do you want to sit down?' he asked politely.

'No, thank you. I have not come to sit down. I have come to remind you, in case you have forgotten, that you have less than two weeks to go. See, I have kept my own part of the deal so far. I have withdrawn my men from the streets. I have allowed TK to be. But I have yet to see any commitment on your part. So I thought I should come to remind you, in case you have forgotten. It is so easy to forget, you know, so easy to break a promise.'

'As you can see, I'm working hard to regain my voice. But my progress has been slow because I have not been able to find TK. He went into hiding after I was arrested, and no one has seen him since.'

'Well, I could go on TV and announce that I have given him a reprieve. Maybe that would encourage him to come out of hiding,' the President suggested.

'I don't think that is a good idea. If you give him a reprieve in a public announcement, and then he comes out to help me make music to praise your government, he would be seen as a sell-out and any music we make will not be well received by the public. Moreover, TK wouldn't have access to a TV in his present circumstances.'

The President thought for a moment. 'You are right,'

he said. 'I will leave it to you. Just remember, you have less than two weeks to deliver.'

'Please don't hurt Lela. I will praise your government with a hit song within two weeks.'

'Well, you know the stakes. But just as a reminder, my men will give you a small dose of hospitality tomorrow. And because I'm a very amenable man, I will send my Negotiator and Mathematician to see you too.'

'Negotiator and Mathematician?' he asked.

The President nodded.

'What have your Negotiator and Mathematician got to do with any of this?'

'You will know when they come to see you tomorrow,' the President replied. 'As I said, I'm a very amenable man. I like giving options to people.' He flashed a dark smile. Then he turned swiftly and was soon lost in the night.

TWENTY-TWO

The limo picked him up in the morning, not long after he returned home from the square where he had rehearsed all night. The presence of the long car drew the attention of his neighbours. But unlike the last time, they refused to come close. Instead, they watched curiously from afar, sensing that something wasn't quite right.

He allowed them to shove him and his guitar into the limo without any struggle. Through the window he saw Aroli hurrying over to see what was amiss. The limo took off in a cloud of dust before Aroli could get to it.

He sank back in the comfortable leather seat, and then he heard quiet snivelling next to him. He turned to look at his companion, and his heart froze when he discovered it was Judah. For a moment he closed his eyes. And then he drew the boy close to him.

'Don't worry, Judah. All will be well.'

Judah continued to cry quietly, frightened that, like his

sister, he may not see his home in a very long time. 'Where are they taking us?' he sobbed.

'What has the boy got to do with any of this?' he shouted at the soldiers who stared morosely at him.

'Don't worry, we won't keep you for long this time. It is going to be a very brief visit,' a soldier said.

'A very brief visit indeed!' he sneered.

'Yes, a very brief visit,' the soldier said patiently. 'We are taking the boy along so he will have more stories to share with his friends. We understand he has been doing a lot of storytelling lately about his last experience. Mr President thought it would be a good idea to give the boy something very nice to say about him.'

'You should be ashamed of yourselves dragging a child into a matter that does not concern him.'

'Watch your mouth!' the soldier snarled.

'Or what?'

'Or I will break your guitar.'

*

They took him to the same underground cell where they kept him last time, while Judah was taken to an unknown destination.

The soldiers stared at him with hostile eyes, and it soon became clear that they were not afraid of his guitar. They were not the same set of soldiers he encountered last time. His new captors spoke in deep-throated voices, like stoned area boys. He watched helplessly as they took his guitar from him before pushing him into the cold cell. He felt defenceless.

'You see, we are not afraid of you,' one soldier taunted him.

He did not respond.

'What can you do now without your guitar?' another asked. 'Answer me!'

He had no answer. He just stared hopelessly at his tormentors.

'Let us know if you need anything,' the first soldier said. 'You are lucky, Mr President instructed us to treat you well. But you might not be so lucky next time.'

He ignored the soldier's threat. 'Where is the boy?' he asked. 'Don't do anything to him, please.'

'Don't worry about the boy. I'm sure he is having fun as we speak. Worry about yourself. Worry about what will happen to you and your girl if Mr President is not happy with you in the end.'

They left him on the cold floor. They closed the gate with a heavy clank and turned off the single bulb. He closed his eyes to shut out the darkness. He could hear the evil echo of their footsteps in the dark endless corridor.

*

He felt completely dejected. The cell grew colder and darker. He was too frightened to attempt to rise from the floor. So he just stayed there in a heap, his eyes fixed on the gate, not knowing what they were planning to do with him this time. He hoped it would not be a repeat of his last experience. Without his guitar it would be unbearable for him. He shivered at the thought of having to stay in that cold cell for days and weeks. And he wondered how Lela had been coping all this time. Given a second chance, he promised himself that he would hasten to praise the regime with a song.

The light was turned on about an hour later, and a soldier came into the cell with food and water. He accepted the food and water to please his captors.

'We want you to be in very good health,' the soldier said as he dropped the food and water on the floor of the cell. 'Eat and drink!' he commanded.

'Thank you,' he replied and ate quietly.

The soldier watched him curiously. What sort of moron would make trouble with Mr President? he was thinking. He shook his head in irritation.

Taduno finished eating and looked up at his captor. 'Thank you,' he said, once again.

'Don't thank me, thank Mr President. Left to me, you will not get anything to eat.'

'Thank Mr President for me,' he responded.

'Now I understand the sort of moron you are,' the soldier said with disbelief, as he picked up the dishes. He clanked the gate shut. Then he turned off the light and left.

*

Darkness engulfed him once again. He slept and woke and slept again. He thought several days had passed since they brought him to that cell. But in fact, it had been only a matter of hours.

He had drifted off to sleep again when the bulb came on, blotting out the darkness in the cell. He rubbed his eyes against the light and sat up eagerly on the floor. A moment later, a soldier opened the gate. And then another soldier dragged Lela in.

She was now a shadow of her former self. She looked disoriented as she stared round the cell, as if she was heavily sedated. Most of her hair had fallen out and her eyes were like black balls in deep holes. He could not believe how badly she had deteriorated since the last time he saw her. He was too shocked to utter a word. He simply stared at her as if she was an apparition conjured in a terrible nightmare. Tears rolled down his cheeks.

He was surprised when Lela focused her eyes upon him and whispered his name. 'Taduno!' Her voice was fierce and gentle at the same time.

Instant hope leapt into his eyes. He scrambled to his feet and ran to her. They embraced silently, and they held on to each other tightly for several moments before a soldier tore them apart.

'We only brought her so that you will see how she is doing. Now we must take her back.'

'Taduno, please help me,' Lela cried out, stretching her hand towards him.

A feeling of desperation gripped him. He told himself he must not allow them to take her away again. He saw that the soldiers carried no guns, and the sudden thought occurred to him to break out of jail with Lela. He had a crazed look in his eyes as he charged at the first soldier and got him down with a swift blow to the head. The second soldier came at him. They exchanged a flurry of punches before locking into a vicious wrestling grip. For several moments they struggled and growled like two wild animals. And then a blow to the back of the head, delivered by the first soldier, knocked Taduno to the floor.

For a while, the soldiers kicked him angrily on the floor, deaf to Lela's pleas and cry of agony.

From a dizzy depth of pain, Taduno heard the gate clank. The light went off. And the departing footsteps soon became distant echoes as they took Lela away.

*

He sat up in a corner of the cell. Even though his entire body was sore with pain, he did not notice. He felt very angry with himself for his failed attempt at jailbreak. He prayed that they would not punish Lela for his action.

He waited.

And then a new set of soldiers with guns and clubs brought in Sergeant Bello. He was the last person Taduno expected them to bring to his cell.

The Sergeant was badly bruised and battered. He kept groaning in agony. His shirt and trousers hung on him in tatters, as if shredded by a lion. He could barely keep his swollen eyes open, and he had to lean on the soldiers who brought him to remain on his feet.

'Somebody help me!' Sergeant Bello moaned, groping in the air with both hands. 'I cannot see!'

'What have you done to him?' Taduno hissed. 'He is an

innocent man.' His anger brought back some of his strength, but he knew better this time.

'He is not innocent,' a soldier replied. 'He confided in someone that he lent his voice to the murmurings of the people. When we interrogated him, he confessed every state secret he sold to you. So you see, he is not an innocent man. He will be charged with treason in the end. And you know that treason is punishable by death.'

'Oh my God,' was all Taduno could whisper.

'We want to extract more information from him. The idea is to get him to identify you as the man he sold government secrets to before taking him back for more interrogation. But unfortunately he has lost his sight.'

Another soldier took over. 'Since he cannot identify you, we would like you to identify him. Do you know this man?' he asked.

Taduno's anguish was too much for him. He hid his face in his hands on the floor of the cell. He became deaf to all their words. He stayed like that until they closed the gate, turned off the light, and took Sergeant Bello away.

TWENTY-THREE

The Negotiator came next, a tall grey man in his late fifties, bent by many years of rigorous negotiations on behalf of an amenable dictator. The man was so grey even his eyebrows were grey, and they stood out stiffly like a trademark that distinguished him from all other species of mankind. Taduno wondered what species of human being he was.

The man came in with a black briefcase. He was smartly dressed in a pinstriped suit and wore rubber-soled shoes that made his approach soundless – the way Negotiators like to walk.

Two plastic chairs were brought into the cell. The man sat down in one, then he nodded to Taduno to take a seat in the other. He obeyed silently, his mind raw with anguish, his body aching. He looked like a man battered by death itself.

'My name is Professor Black,' the man introduced himself. 'I am a negotiator and I'm here to see you on behalf of Mr President. I believe you are already aware of my coming.'

Taduno nodded indifferently.

'Good. My job is to put Mr President's options on the table before you. After I have done that, Mr President's Mathematician will come to help you make what I will call a crucial mathematical decision. Then I will come back to help you and Mr President reach a mutually beneficial agreement. I hope I have made myself clear?'

'Not exactly. But please go ahead. I'm listening.'

'Very good!' Professor Black clapped his hands with satisfaction. He opened his briefcase, brought out several sheets of paper and made a big deal of going through them, adjusting his glasses precariously on the edge of his nose. Minutes later, he looked up from the papers in his hand, took off his glasses and fixed a soft gaze upon Taduno. 'Mr President wants to make you an offer,' he said.

'An offer? Why does he want to make me an offer?'

'Because he is a very amenable man. In fact, he wants to be your friend. He likes you a lot and thinks you are a very intelligent man. If you ask me, I would say he is a very loyal friend.'

Taduno sighed. He could tell that Professor Black was a very seasoned negotiator indeed, his grey personality a testimony to how well he had done over the years. He shook his head. 'I still do not understand why he wants to make me an offer. And what offer does he want to make me? Even if he makes me an offer, he is known to be a man who never keeps his word.'

'Look, this time he will keep his word. I will spell it

out for you. He is prepared to make you the richest musician alive.'

Taduno frowned. 'I don't understand. He is holding my girlfriend hostage. Why would he want to make me rich?'

'You see, Mr President is worried that you might be stubborn enough to let your girlfriend die by going back on the promise you made him. So he has decided to show why he is such an amenable man. He is offering to make you a very rich man if you agree to praise his government with your music. He wants you to name your price, any amount, in addition to having your girlfriend released.'

'But I have already agreed to make music to praise his government,' Taduno said, a frown still on his face.

'We know that. But what if you are not being sincere? What if you are planning to ambush the government by going contrary to your promise? He is a soldier, see? A soldier does not take his adversary for granted. That is why he wants to make you an offer you cannot refuse.'

'I don't need a penny from him. Let him release my girlfriend. And Sergeant Bello too. That's all I need.'

Professor Black raised a hand sharply. 'If you say another word about Sergeant Bello this whole deal will be off!' His voice was dead serious. 'Regarding Mr President's offer to make you a rich man, do not make a hurried decision yet. I will leave you for a moment. Mr President's Mathematician will come to see you and help you understand the infinite riches that could be yours. I will come back when he is done and then we can finish this discussion.' He rose and left the cell.

*

To Taduno's surprise, the President's Mathematician was a young man in his early twenties. He wore nerdy glasses that complemented his looks perfectly. He came in with a calculator as big as a laptop, the like of which Taduno had never seen before and would never see again.

He walked into the cell as if Taduno was not there and took the seat the Negotiator had just vacated. He adjusted his glasses carefully, took his time to turn on the calculator, and then he looked up and acknowledged Taduno's presence with a faint smile.

'My name is Professor Ajao. I'm a young professor of mathematics.' He introduced himself with the haughtiness of a man who had made it too early in life. Then he used the same line as Professor Black – 'I believe you are already aware of my coming' – an indication that he too must have been working for the President for a while.

Taduno nodded. 'Yes, I'm aware of your coming, young professor of mathematics,' he said morosely.

'Very good!' Professor Ajao said. 'I am here to help you understand the multiplying power of the number zero. You see, most people have the erroneous belief that zero is worthless. But I will prove to you just how very wrong they are.' He paused and laughed. 'In actual fact, zero is by far more powerful than all other numbers.'

'How?' Taduno asked, wondering where the conversation was leading.

'Very good question! Without wasting any more of your time, I'm going to ask you to perform a simple task for me, if you don't mind, please,' the Mathematician said. Then he punched '1' on the calculator and handed it to Taduno.

'What am I supposed to do with this?'

'I have typed one into the calculator. May I ask you to add a zero to the one, please?'

Taduno shrugged and complied.

'And another zero, please?'

Again Taduno complied.

'And another . . . and another . . . and another . . . and another . . .' On and on the Mathematician went until Taduno had typed in so many zeros his head began to spin.

Finally, the Mathematician sat back with a smile on his face. 'What is the final figure you have?' he asked.

Taduno looked down at the calculator in his hands. He tried to count the zeros, but a mist swarmed him. The more he tried to count the zeros, the longer they became.

'What is the final figure?' the Mathematician persisted, the smile still on his face.

'The zeros are too many,' Taduno replied. 'I cannot pronounce the exact figure.'

'Very good!' The smile broadened on the face of the Mathematician. 'That's how rich Mr President wants to make you. My task is done. Think about it.' And with that he rose and walked briskly out of the cell.

He left Taduno gaping at the giant calculator.

*

The Negotiator returned immediately. He seemed in a hurry this time, and he did not open his briefcase to bring out the mysterious sheets of paper he had studied earlier. 'I believe you have been told just how rich Mr President wants to make you?' he asked.

'Yes,' Taduno replied, looking down at the calculator in his hands, his head still reeling from how many zeros he had added to one.

'So, I ask you to mention any figure you can imagine, any figure at all, and Mr President will have it paid into your account within twenty-four hours in exchange for making a hit song to praise his government. In addition, your girlfriend will be released.'

Taduno took a deep breath. 'Please pass this message to your client for me. Tell him I don't want a penny from him. Tell him I have agreed to praise his government with my music. And that's about it. I don't want a penny from him, all I want is Lela. And I hope I have made myself very clear.' He reached over and dumped the calculator with all the weight of its zeros into the lap of the Negotiator.

The Negotiator shrugged. Looking down at the calculator on his lap, his head spun with the infinite possibilities of wealth represented by the countless zeros that stared back at him. He bit his lip. 'Have it your way. But I must remind you, the freedom of your girl is in your hands. As for Sergeant Bello, forget him.' He left the cell with his briefcase and the giant calculator.

*

His ego terribly bruised, the Negotiator did what he had never done before – he sought help, and returned about an hour later in the company of the Central Bank Governor, a willowy man in a flowing white gown who smelled of freshly minted money. Taduno was balled up on the floor in a corner of the cell. He had been balled up like that for nearly an hour. He rose gingerly to his feet as the bulb came on and his two visitors walked in.

'I had to come back, seeing we could not reach an agreement earlier,' the Negotiator said, with a weak smile.

'It is pointless coming back, I do not intend to change my mind,' Taduno replied bluntly, his eyes fixed on the Governor, wondering why he had come with the Negotiator.

'I believe we can reach an agreement with the right offer,' the Negotiator replied, trying to sound confident.

'Please do not waste your time, and do not waste my time, I beg of you.'

The Negotiator ignored his plea. 'Permit me to introduce you to the Governor.'

'I know who he is,' Taduno replied without interest. Turning to the Governor, he said, 'Welcome to my cold cell, Governor, I hope you find it comfortable enough.'

The willowy man gave him a generous smile. 'You do not deserve to be in a cold cell, that's why I'm here. I'm sure we can resolve this whole matter peacefully.'

'I probably deserve to be in a hot cell,' Taduno said with a sarcastic laugh, 'a hot mosquito-infested cell. Yes, that's what I deserve.'

'No, you do not deserve to be in any cell at all,' the Governor replied patiently, gently. 'This is a mistake that will soon be resolved, I assure you.'

Taduno eyed him without a word.

'He came to see you with a message from Mr President,' the Negotiator put in smoothly.

'And what's the message?'

'We will get to that, but first let us make ourselves comfortable.' The Negotiator had turned on his charms.

Three plastic chairs were brought into the cell, at the request of the Negotiator. The chairs were arranged in the middle of the cell, under the bulb. They made themselves comfortable, and the Governor got straight to business.

'Mr President is offering you the opportunity to own your own money,' the man said with a broad smile.

'I don't understand,' Taduno said.

'In exchange for supporting his government with your music, he is offering you this note,' the Governor said, bringing a crisp 500-naira note out of his garment and holding it up for Taduno to see.

Taduno laughed. 'He is offering me five hundred naira to sell my soul?' he asked incredulously. 'Five hundred naira to sell the people of my country?'

'Oh no, not so!' The Governor smiled. 'He is offering you the opportunity to have your face on a new five hundred-naira bill – the opportunity to own your own money! If you agree to the deal, you can order any amount of this note to be printed and delivered to you as frequently as you like. Any amount at all!'

'You will never have to worry for money again as long as you live,' the Negotiator added eagerly.

'And I may only live for one day after agreeing to the deal,' Taduno said, with a bitter laugh.

'The Almighty gives and takes life as He pleases,' the

Governor said meekly. 'If you live for only one day after agreeing to the deal, to God be the glory. And if you live a hundred years, to God Almighty be the glory. I'll give you my personal advice – take the deal with both hands.'

'You will never get a better offer!' The Negotiator's voice was anxious.

'I'm not interested,' Taduno said curtly. 'I will make the music, I promise, but not for money. Now please leave my cell!' His tone of voice left no room for negotiation.

The two men exchanged baffled looks and rose as one to their feet. Too stunned to say another word, they left the cell in defeat. The Negotiator had never failed an assignment so miserably before.

*

They released him and his guitar at 7 p.m., after eleven hours of incarceration. But they did not take him home in the limo. Instead, they dumped him opposite army headquarters with enough money to catch a taxi home.

'You know what you must do now,' a soldier said to him in a cold voice. 'Time is no longer on your side.'

Yes, he knew what he must do now. But he had to make sure Judah was okay first. He caught a taxi straight to the boy's house.

To his relief, he found Judah in his parents' compound, surrounded by several of his friends. He was recounting his latest experience to them in an even more excited voice than he had the last time. He broke off his story and jumped to his feet to greet Taduno.

'Are you okay, Judah?' he asked, studying the boy's face.

'Yes, I'm okay, Uncle Taduno.'

'What did they do to you?'

'They took me to the President. He was very nice to me. He gave me ice cream and popcorn and we watched *Tom and Jerry* together on the biggest TV I have ever seen! And then they brought me home in the long car!'

'I'm glad you are okay,' Taduno mumbled.

'The President was so nice to me,' the boy continued. 'He kept smiling and telling me that all will be okay. He told me *Anti* Lela will be home soon!'

'Yes, your sister will be home soon.' He ruffled the boy's hair. 'Now I must leave you to continue with your story. I have to attend to an urgent matter.' A deep sigh escaped him.

He could not blame the boy. He was still too young to understand. All that mattered was his sister's release. Nothing else mattered. Why should anything else matter?

What remained of Taduno's conscience died that day, and he sensed that only with the death of his conscience would he be able to sing beautifully once again.

*

It was already night. He saw no reason to go home. Instead, he took a bus directly to TBS where he found the homeless men already gathered, anxiously waiting for him. They cheered his arrival loudly.

'Thank God you came!' Thaddeus said happily.

'I had to come,' he replied.

191

He had no time to waste. As the soldier had reminded him, time was no longer on his side. He settled down in the midst of the homeless men and began to play his guitar.

On this night, unlike other nights, he sang slowly along to the tune of his guitar. He sang with simplicity, with a passion too colourful for words. And to his surprise and that of his listeners, his voice hit the beautiful note that once made him the greatest musician of his time.

The homeless men were delirious with joy. A thunderous applause resounded in the square when he finished singing. He rose up to milk the applause. It did not matter that he was now ready to betray an entire nation. What mattered was that he would be saving the woman he loved from a ruthless dictator. 'Why should anything else matter?' This was now his watchword.

Not until the applause had died down did he realise that Aroli was in the midst of the homeless men. The two of them embraced amidst the excited chatter that now gripped the square.

'You have discovered your voice at last!' Aroli exclaimed with delight.

He smiled. 'It's about time!'

'I'm glad I came tonight to witness this.'

Thaddeus slapped him on the back. 'Boy, you did that in style! That was pure magic!'

'All of you provided me with the inspiration. I thank you all.' He sounded like he meant the words, but deep down in his heart, he knew he had got the ultimate inspiration from the anguish he saw on Lela's face earlier that day, and the pathetic fate of Sergeant Bello.

'Now what?' Thaddeus asked.

'Now I'm ready to make music again.'

It no longer disturbed his conscience that he would be making music to praise a tyrant. As far as he was concerned, music is music. Why should anything else matter?

He did not need to rehearse at the far end of the square any more. He returned home with Aroli that night.

*

'It is good to be back home,' he said, when they got to his house, way past midnight.

He inhaled deeply. And then he placed his guitar in a corner.

'I'm glad they didn't keep you for so long this time,' Aroli said. 'I saw them take you away. What happened? Where did they take you?'

'To the cell under the underground cell,' he replied. 'The same place they took me last time.' He went on to tell Aroli about his latest encounter with Lela and the tragic fate of Sergeant Bello.

Aroli raised his hand to his mouth. 'Oh my God!' he whispered to himself. 'Is there anything that can be done to save him?'

'I tried, but it was useless.'

'What is the next step?'

'I am ready to praise the regime with my music. I cannot allow Lela to continue to suffer in their hands. I feel very certain now that they will not hesitate to kill her.'

'I agree. But how are you going to go about producing the music without TK?'

'Fortunately, I have to do it without TK. It is too dirty a job for TK. I know the right man for the job.'

'Who?'

'Mr Player.'

Aroli nodded. 'He will be very delighted to sign you. When do we go to see him?'

'You mean when do I go to see him?'

Aroli sighed. 'I don't think this is something you should do on your own.'

'It is something I must do on my own. I don't want to drag you into my dirty business.'

Again Aroli sighed. 'When are you going to see him?'

'Tomorrow.'

'Let me know how things develop.'

'I will.'

They stayed in silence.

'I'm on the verge of sealing a big property deal,' Aroli announced, after a while. 'It is the deal of my life, enough to help me retire and become a full-time poet.'

'I'm happy for you!' Taduno could not contain his excitement. 'At long last!'

'Yes, at long last. I'll seal the deal in a few days.'

'This deserves a toast surely!'

They had a few bottles of beer in the kitchen while Aroli told him all about the mega-deal that had fallen into his lap so miraculously.

TWENTY-FOUR

Taduno arrived at the Studio of Stars at about ten, and he received a rousing welcome. Many of the people he knew no longer worked there; but everyone knew him. The female secretary, who happened to be a new staff member, ushered him into Mr Player's office with pride, her pretty face flushed.

Mr Player was overjoyed to see him. He rose from his desk to welcome him with open arms, apologising profusely about the last time.

'Sorry, I did not remember you the last time you were here. It still does not make sense to me. I cannot explain what happened!' Mr Player sounded genuinely baffled.

'It's okay,' Taduno said. 'Everyone forgot me. I guess it is just one of those things that cannot be explained.'

Mr Player's face deepened into a frown, still trying to understand. And then he shook his head helplessly. 'What brings you here?'

Taduno saw no point beating about the bush. 'I want to sign for your label,' he said solemnly.

Silence fell, and for several moments Mr Player simply stared at him. Thinking he did not hear him correctly, he asked, 'What did you say?'

Taduno repeated himself.

Mr Player let out a howl of joy. He jumped to his feet and went round his desk to hug Taduno, almost pushing him down to the floor in the process.

'Of course I would be delighted to sign you!' Mr Player said, after managing to rein in his emotion.

Taduno continued with his very direct approach. 'I want to produce a hit song within the next week to praise the President and his government,' he explained.

Mr Player was stunned. Not that the idea troubled him; in fact, he saw it as the perfect opportunity to make the kind of money any producer can only dream of. He beamed. 'I'm in favour of praising government with music!' he said.

'We must get it on the airwaves and into every record shop in ten days.' Taduno hesitated and added, with a hint of desperation, 'It is urgent. There is no time to waste.'

And then Mr Player smelled a rat. 'What can be so urgent about producing music to praise the President?' he asked.

'Because it is very urgent,' Taduno replied lamely, not wanting to explain his precarious position. 'Rest assured it will be worth your while.'

Mr Player's business mind took over. It occurred to him that Taduno must be getting something for praising the President and that something must be an unimaginable amount of money. His mind began to race with excitement. It was an opportunity too good to miss.

'Are you telling me that you have the President's approval to undertake this project?' Mr Player asked.

'Yes, he commissioned it.'

'Any written agreement?' He wanted to be sure that he was undertaking the right investment.

'Take me at my word.'

Mr Player thought for a moment. He could hear his own brain ticking. Ordinarily, he would have taken Taduno at his word. But he reasoned that if Taduno was willing to stoop so low to praise a dictator with his music, then he was no longer a man to be trusted. So, he told himself to secure his investment before agreeing to anything.

'What is in it for me?' Mr Player asked.

Taduno frowned. 'What did you say?'

'I said what is in it for me?'

'I'm sure Mr President will make it worth your while when the music is out.' His heart raced with anxiety.

'I'm sorry, that is not good enough for me.' Mr Player shook his head. 'I'm a businessman, see? I have to know what I'm getting. It doesn't come cheap to praise a tyrant with music – good music for that matter. I want a percentage of what you are getting. Forty per cent. And I think that is a fair deal.'

Taduno almost blurted out that he was getting nothing – apart from securing the release of his girlfriend. But he realised that that would put Mr Player off.

'I will see to it that you get something from Mr President,' he said hopelessly.

'No!' Mr Player said sharply. 'I have no business with the President. My business is with you. I want forty per cent of what you get. And I want to see something in writing telling me how much you are getting from Mr President.'

'Getting something in writing could prove difficult,' Taduno croaked.

'Those are my conditions. If you give me what I want, we will have the music out in less than a week.'

Mr Player rose to his feet.

'Take me at my word,' Taduno pleaded.

Mr Player shook his head. He wanted to say, 'Given the level you have descended to, your word counts for nothing.' But he simply shook his head again.

The meeting was over.

*

Taduno roamed the streets in confusion, acknowledging half-heartedly the greetings that followed him. His guitar was a heavy weight on his shoulder and he thought of flinging it away and telling the President to go to hell. But he remembered Lela's words, and he knew he could not afford to do something so rash.

Time wasn't on Lela's side. Every passing second increased the possibility of her dying in detention. He needed to make urgent contact with the President, but he had no way of doing so. He agonised under the fiercely burning sun. His lips were parched. His mind became blurred. And then as he walked past a lone soldier, a brazen idea suddenly occurred to him.

Without wasting any time, he caught a taxi to army headquarters.

*

He arrived at army headquarters playing a loud meaning-less tune on his guitar and a handful of soldiers promptly swarmed around him, shouting angry orders to stop his useless music. And then, realising who he was, they stepped back and warily trained their guns on him.

'What brings you and your music here?' a soldier asked.

'I have come to be arrested,' he responded.

The soldiers exchanged curious glances.

'Why do you want to be arrested?'

'Because I want to see the President.'

Again the soldiers exchanged glances.

'Mr President is a busy man. He cannot see you! And we have orders not to arrest or maltreat you.'

'In that case his government will be toppled! And all of you will go down with him!'

Gripped by fear, the soldiers took the only logical action open to them. They arrested him.

A smile of triumph lit up Taduno's face.

*

They bundled him through the gates without bothering to search him or confiscate his guitar. No one wanted to touch his guitar. They saw it as a very deadly weapon that

199

must not be touched – a weapon capable of overthrowing the President.

News quickly spread throughout army headquarters that the government was about to be overthrown. The army chief gave hurried instructions and all military bases were placed on red alert. The stampede that followed reverberated in far and distant regions.

They processed him through the ranks until he stood before the army chief who was not sure how to handle him and his guitar. 'What are your demands?' the man asked, too confused to think straight.

'I have just one. Take me to the President. Or else he will be toppled and all of you will go down with him.'

Not unaware of the President's desperate efforts to buy Taduno over, the army chief sensed that the situation was very serious indeed. And so, without uttering another word, he took him before the President.

*

The President welcomed him warmly. 'To what do I owe this visit?' he asked, after dismissing the army chief.

'I have a problem,' he replied, 'a problem that could derail our earlier arrangement.'

For a brief moment the President's face hardened. 'And what is this problem?'

Taduno explained.

The President thought for a moment. 'That can be fixed,' he said with a smile. 'Shouldn't be difficult at all.' He called in the army chief and told him what to do. 'I want Mr Player brought here immediately. And make sure you treat him very nicely.'

*

They brought in Mr Player within the hour. He looked terribly agitated, but relaxed a little when he saw Taduno and the President chatting lightly like old friends. He could not believe his eyes.

'Please take a seat,' the President said. His charm put Mr Player completely at ease.

'Thank you, Mr President,' Mr Player replied, sitting down.

'My friend here explained everything to me. He said you are asking for forty per cent of whatever he gets and that you want a written commitment from me.'

'That's because I wasn't so sure you commissioned the project yourself, Mr President. But now that I'm sure, there's no problem at all. The song will be out in less than a week. And it will be on the airwaves and in all record shops.'

'Good!' the President beamed. 'I have no problem with you getting forty per cent of whatever Taduno gets. To me that is okay. But there's a slight problem because I don't know how much Taduno wants. But as the three of us are here, we might as well settle that.'

Mr Player nodded eagerly. 'I agree, Mr President. It makes good sense to me!'

'So how much do you want?' the President asked, turning to Taduno.

'Nothing. I want nothing,' Taduno replied.

Mr Player's jaw dropped.

'So you get forty per cent of nothing,' the President said, with a delighted clap of his hands.

'But, Mr President . . .' Mr Player stammered.

'Relax! I can understand your shock,' the President said with a laugh. 'You get forty per cent of nothing from Taduno. And from me, to show my gratitude, you will get seven truckloads of money. How about that?'

A smile spread across Mr Player's face. 'That sounds perfect, Mr President! Very perfect!'

'Good. So we have a deal?'

'Yes, Mr President, we have a deal!' Mr Player rubbed his palms together, a very grateful man.

'Come to think of it . . .' the President said with some thought.

'Yes, Mr President?'

'I think you should do a concert before releasing the song into the market. The national stadium would be a perfect venue. That will make the song popular, don't you think?'

'Yes, Mr President,' Mr Player nodded, 'it makes a lot of sense.' The deal was getting better!

'Great, so Taduno plays at the national stadium a day before the song is released.'

'Yes, Mr President!'

Taduno was speechless.

The President turned to him. 'Deal?'

He was trapped, he simply nodded.

The President smiled.

And so the matter was settled. The red alert was eased across the country, and relief rose into the air from every military base.

Back at the studio, a contract was hastily drawn up and signed, including the clause that Mr Player would receive forty per cent of nothing from Taduno. Mr Player kept apologising for not taking Taduno at his word. 'You know, you can never be too careful when it comes to business,' he said.

'I understand.' Taduno's voice was flat.

'When can you report to the studio to start work? I say we start immediately!'

'I will report in two days. I have an assignment to carry out before then.'

Mr Player shrugged. 'I'll be right here waiting!'

TWENTY-FIVE

Taduno was in a very sober mood as he went about his assignment the following day. At Mama Iyabo's restaurant, he held a concert that drew a large crowd that covered the entire street. He delivered a scintillating performance, a Farewell to Conscience. His audience wailed in adulation and stretched their hands towards him, grateful that he was singing with a magnetic voice once again.

From Mama Iyabo's restaurant, Taduno went round the famous bus stops of the city, enchanting delirious crowds with hit performances. Aroli and Vulcaniser followed him as he went, and they both agreed that they had never seen him perform so brilliantly before. But while Aroli understood what was to follow – the death his voice would undergo – Vulcaniser was merely left to wonder.

The Channel 4 newscaster beamed with joy. Her station aired Taduno's performances live; her background commentary pulsated with colourful words. 'Taduno is back with a bang!' she screamed with delight. 'The people have a voice once again! Music, rare music, joyous music is back into our lives!' On and on she went, her words rolling out with polished diction.

In his office, the President watched with satisfaction, his manicured fingers caressing a paper knife. He had always wanted Taduno to sing in praise of his government. Now his wish was about to come true! He saw no better way to get legitimacy, no better man to give him legitimacy.

*

Taduno brought his performance to a grand closure at TBS. It was not only the homeless men that were present at the square that night; people from all walks of life came too. Even the President's men, caught under the spell of his music once again, came without their guns.

The crowd covered the square and beyond, with barely space for anyone to move an inch. A giant podium had been hastily set up for him. And when he climbed onto it, even before he strummed his guitar or opened his mouth to sing, a deafening roar of approval that lasted several minutes shook the city. Absolute silence ensued. Then the first notes from his guitar tore through the night. His voice followed, and the crowd began to heave with a joy that even the Channel 4 newscaster could not describe with words.

The concert ended at midnight although the audience wanted it to go on for ever. But he had to bring it to an end so that he could spend one last night alone at his far end of the square.

At last, only Aroli, Vulcaniser and the homeless men remained. Everyone came forward to congratulate him on his brilliant performance. Aroli and Vulcaniser wanted to stay with him at the square, but he begged them to go home, and they did as he asked.

After Aroli and Vulcaniser had gone, Thaddeus came over to hug him before retiring to bed. 'Good night and good luck, my friend,' he said.

Taduno waited until loud snoring filled the square. He listened to the snorers as he had always listened to them. He smiled as he listened to them. He knew he was going to miss them dearly. For one last time, he imagined them as they were before they became homeless. He hoped that they would remember him by his performance that night and not by the ones that would follow.

*

He was ready to retire to his far end of the square when he saw a squat figure walking slowly towards him. He did not need to squint into the night to know it was TK. He dropped his head with a deep sigh and remained like that until the approaching man sat next to him. Somehow, he sensed it was time to say goodbye.

'I see you have discovered your voice at last,' TK said.

Only then did Taduno raise his head to look at TK. He looked so different without his Afro. In fact, according to Thaddeus, he looked as if he was no longer of this world. A cold hand clutched Taduno's heart.

'Yes, I'm ready to sing again.'

'And I suppose your priority is to save Lela.'

'Yes,' he replied, sadness in his voice.

A moment of silence passed between them.

'Don't do it, Taduno. Please don't do it,' TK pleaded in a low voice. 'Don't praise the tyrant with your music.'

'I have no choice.'

'Yes, you have a choice.'

'No, I have none. As long as they have Lela I have no choice. I must save her, and the only way is to praise the regime with my music. If I don't, they will kill her.'

'They can only kill her once,' TK said patiently. 'But if you praise the regime with your music you will be signing the death warrant of millions of people.' He paused. 'Which do you prefer?'

Taduno did not answer. Instead, he said, 'I have signed a contract with Mr Player. I'm reporting to the studio in the morning.'

'So there is no going back?'

'TK, please understand. There is no other way.'

'There is always another way.'

'Which way?' Taduno turned to look at him.

'The way of a miracle. A miracle could happen – just as it has happened for Aroli, after all these years.'

'What do you mean?'

'He has struck a big property deal and can now retire to his dream job.'

'How did you know?' Taduno could not hide his surprise.

'A deal like that is too big to be done quietly. It is all over the papers. It is almost as big as a miracle can be.'

They fell into silence again.

TK spoke after a lengthy interval. 'So you see, there's always the possibility of a miracle. But you must show faith to receive it.'

Not knowing what to say, Taduno told TK about Sergeant Bello. 'It looks like the man has lost his sight,' he said. 'They told me he will face the death sentence.'

'That's another reason why you should not praise the tyrant with your music. If you do, you will be endorsing Sergeant Bello's fate. And you will turn yourself into one of his persecutors. We must not select those to save and those to condemn to death in the fight against tyranny. We must learn to say "no" to tyrants no matter how much they hurt us. That is the only way tyranny can be defeated.'

Taduno remained silent.

TK continued. 'This is the last time we will meet. My parting message to you is show some faith. A miracle will come.' With those words TK rose to his feet and walked away.

Taduno could not stop him, or even call out to him. He felt very sad as he watched him leave.

*

He no longer wanted to sleep at the square that night, so he returned home. As he opened his door, he noticed a stained brown envelope on the doormat. He noticed that the stains on the envelope were much heavier than on the envelopes he had received in the past. His heart pounded as he bent down to pick it up. He opened the

208

letter as soon as he entered the house. And he read it eagerly, standing in the middle of the living room.

— — —

Dear Taduno,
I hope this letter finds you. I beg you not to praise tyranny with your music.

Don't worry about me, I will be OK. After all, the whole world is a prison, the only difference being that some live inside prison while others live outside prison, but prison all the same. So I will be OK.

Sing that song. And as you do, I pledge you my undying love . . .

Always,
Lela

His heart ached for Lela by the time he finished reading knowing that he must revoke his contract with Mr Player. He got drunk in the upper room, with his hit songs of yesteryear echoing in his mind. And he slept on the bare floor, amongst sad and silent shadows.

TWENTY-SIX

Morning came quickly. Taduno shook off his hangover with two more drinks, without a song in his soul, and then his mind became very clear, and he remembered that he had taken the decision to condemn Lela to her fate.

He could no longer sing for love and no longer had the strength to sing against tyranny. And now that he was free of all responsibilities and worries, he saw only one future ahead of him – a life at the square beside his dear friend Thaddeus.

He had always known it, that there was something about him and Thaddeus – something that linked them together. He imagined the public snorers, and he realised that it was inevitable that his own snoring would one day complement theirs in the grand symphony of their sad songs. Now he was set to make a different kind of music – one that would denounce love.

*

He packed everything he could possibly need. He packed some clothes and shoes for Thaddeus too. He packed his cooking pots and plates and spoons. He almost forgot his old coffee mugs! He would need those to drink coffee with Thaddeus while they sit together and try to count the stars beneath the night sky of the square. Who knows, they might be able to achieve the feat together one day. He felt a tingle of excitement.

The President can go to hell now, Mr Player too, and all the villains who drive dreamers to the square. He no longer had to worry about them or anyone else. In fact, he no longer had to worry about himself.

He had just finished packing the last bag when Aroli came knocking, as loud as ever. He wasn't startled; he had passed the point where anything or anyone could startle him. He would soon be lost among the homeless men at the square and not even the President would ever be able to find him again. He would forget Aroli, Vulcaniser and Judah. Only memories of Lela would remain, and it would be those memories that would confine him to the square.

'You are sweating,' Aroli said, as he walked in.

'Yes, I am sweating,' he replied, going up the stairs to his bedroom.

Aroli followed him, and he was shocked when he saw all the bags on the floor. 'What are these?' he asked.

'My bags,' he replied. 'I'm leaving.'

Aroli could not believe his ears. 'You're leaving?'

'Yes.'

'Leaving to where?'

'To TBS. I'm going to join my friend Thaddeus and the rest. I'm going to live with them.'

Aroli frowned. 'Let's get this straight. Since when did Thaddeus become a friend you want to go and live with?'

'What I mean is I'm no longer going to praise the regime with my music. I will let Lela die, and I'm going to live at the square for ever where the dictator or anyone can never find me again. I will be a free man at the square, without worries or responsibilities.'

Aroli was lost for what to say. He stared hard at the floor, and when he looked up and opened his mouth to speak, he knew it was pointless. Taduno had made up his mind. Nothing he said would change anything. He wished he could take the place of his friend, and bear the pain he must now bear for the rest of his life. He wished he could do something to change things, but he knew he was powerless to do anything.

They held each other in a long embrace, each trying to hide his tears. Then Aroli helped him to get his bags outside where the people of that street soon gathered. 'What is happening?' 'Where are you going?' 'Are you leaving us?' They asked many questions but got no answer in return, just silence. Vulcaniser was the only one who did not say a word; he just stood there, gazing into space.

After they brought out the last bag, Taduno flagged down a taxi. Vulcaniser and Aroli loaded his bags into the taxi. And as the taxi drove him away, Aroli and all the rest of his neighbours broke down and wept in the street.

Judah was not there to see him leave.

He had Lela's last letter in his breast pocket. He cradled his guitar to his chest in the back seat of the yellow taxi. It was too early for him to show up at the square, so he told the driver to drive aimlessly around the city for a while. The man complied with a smile, grateful for the privilege to drive Taduno around the city. He would never tire to tell his grandchildren of the day he drove the greatest musician around Lagos.

'Sir, is there anything you particularly want to see?' the driver asked, studying the face of his famous fare in the rear-view mirror.

'Yes, one last time I want to see the city as it truly is because I might never get the opportunity to do so again,' he replied, trying to sound cheerful.

'Oh, I see. Are you going away somewhere?'

'Yes, I'm going away. I'm going where no one can ever find me.'

'What about your music? What'll happen to your music?'

'Truly, I don't know. I don't know what will happen to my music.' There was a slight trembling in his voice.

The driver did not know what to say. He fixed his eyes intently on the road, afraid that he could lose his way in the city he had lived in all his life.

*

Taduno saw the city again as he saw it before, through the words of his songs. He saw the infernal struggles of the people, which by far outweighed their greatest rewards. He saw their fear and pain and the hopelessness that drove them on, round the clock. And as he saw these things, he knew he must not condemn them further by praising tyranny with his song. He must let Lela die, and for that he must live at the square for the rest of his life.

For him, the square would become a purgatory. But it wouldn't be so bad a place. He would have Thaddeus for company, and they would busy themselves counting stars every night and drinking coffee in his old mugs. As the time inched past seven, he leaned forward and tapped the driver gently on the shoulder.

'You may head for TBS now,' he said in a quiet voice.

*

They welcomed him with open arms at the square, and they assigned him a special sleeping place amongst them. Thaddeus helped him to settle in. Taduno unpacked his things and gave Thaddeus the clothes and shoes he brought him.

'Thank you,' Thaddeus said.

He bought food from a roadside restaurant, and all of them, about fifty in number, ate as a family. The grace was said by Thaddeus, and the 'amen' that followed was quiet and humbling. They ate thoughtfully, and when they finished they spent some time belching their satisfaction. Then they thanked Taduno for his kindness. They didn't want to burden him by requesting him to play them his music, but of course life at the square would be more

214

interesting with music. He understood; he was a very understanding man. So, without any prompting he picked up his guitar and they all gathered around him. And as the first strains of his song filtered into the night, their oily lips parted in faint smiles. Life wasn't so bad at the square after all!

But how long will the good time last? This question tugged at each one of them.

*

When the rest had gone to bed, he and Thaddeus made themselves coffee in the old mugs, and they sat on a bench with their faces gazing up at the night sky with its millions of brilliant stars.

'How many stars do you think are up there?' he asked Thaddeus.

'At the last count I hit two million five hundred and sixty, and I'm still counting!' Thaddeus replied proudly.

'Oh boy!' he whistled. 'I have some catching up to do seeing as I have to start from one.'

'I started from one too, and see where I am today! All you have to do is start and you will be surprised how rapid your progress will be. Don't worry, I will be here to guide you, to encourage you.'

Taduno nodded thankfully.

They sat back. Taduno started counting from one; Thaddeus continued from where he had stopped.

*

He had never known the real meaning of 'drifting' before. But he came to understand it as Thaddeus showed him round the following day. By daytime the square was a completely different place, with countless tourists coming and going. To his surprise, the section of the square which they made their home was off-limits to the tourists. The men worked in shifts to patrol its precincts, making sure no intruder came into their domain.

They were an organised and principled bunch. They stole from no one and no one stole from them. When not on patrol duty, each was free to take the day off to drift around the city and do any menial job they could find.

Thaddeus showed him the extent of the square, which was far bigger than he previously thought. They walked amongst the tourists, with tattered fedoras covering their faces, ensuring their anonymity. He did not carry his guitar with him. Thaddeus assured him that it was safe in his new home.

They ate breakfast and then lunch at bustling roadside restaurants, and they spent the rest of the day generally roaming the square. It was a different kind of experience for him. Tiring maybe, but this was his life now, and he told himself he must get used to it.

He did not bother to look out for TK. He knew he had lost him for ever. He believed him when he said they would never meet again. No doubt, he would miss TK terribly, but, gratefully, Thaddeus was proving to be a very good friend.

It was a very hot day, and as the heat increased, more

216

and more people thronged the square to wait for the breeze
that would arrive at nightfall to dry their sweat.

*

Taduno was furious when Aroli showed up with Mr Player
that night. He was already beginning to get used to his
new life at the square, even beginning to enjoy it. And
then Aroli showed up, just like that.

Without thinking, he grabbed Aroli by the neck and
shook him with the full force of his rage until some of his
friends grabbed him and pulled him away.

'You could kill him!' Thaddeus reprimanded him.

'He has no business bringing anyone here to see me!'

'Remember, he is your friend.'

'What friend would give his friend away?'

'Calm down,' Thaddeus said, placing a gentle hand on
his shoulder. 'Calm down, see what he has to say.'

He took a few deep breaths, and then his rage subsided.

'I'm sorry,' Aroli said, holding a hand to his neck.

'Why did you bring him here?'

'He came to look for you. He said it was very urgent, a
matter of life and death. I had no choice but to bring him
to you. I'm sorry, I didn't know you would be so upset.'

'I'm sorry for choking you.'

'Trying to kill me, you mean,' Aroli said with a laugh.
They embraced warmly.

Mr Player cleared his throat beside them. 'Taduno, please
come with me. It is important that we talk.'

Even though he wasn't happy to see Mr Player, he knew

217

he must listen to what he had to say. So he followed him into the night, away from the others.

*

'Why didn't you show up at the studio as agreed? And why did you come to live here?' Mr Player asked.

'Because I no longer want to make music to praise a tyrant,' he responded plainly.

'Have you taken time to think about the consequences of your action? Have you thought about what Mr President can do to you?'

'I haven't and I don't care.'

Mr Player shook his head. 'What about Lela?'

'What about her?' There was fear in his voice. 'How did you know about Lela? Who told you?'

'After the meeting we had with Mr President, he sent for me and he explained your predicament to me.'

'The bastard!'

'He said the reason why you don't want any money from him is because you want to secure Lela's release instead. Are you going let her die now?'

'Yes, I will let her die if that will save me from praising tyranny with my music. They can only kill her once. They cannot kill her twice.'

Mr Player laughed, a pitiful laughter.

'You don't know what you are saying. Do you think they are just going to put a bullet into her head and kill her just like that? My dear friend, you are wrong. They will kill her slowly, very slowly. They could take up to a year, even more, to kill her. That's not the kind of death you wish a loved one.'

Taduno shivered at Mr Player's words.

'I advise that you report to the studio tomorrow to make the song that will save your girl's life. For your information, Mr President is already making arrangements. He plans to fill the national stadium with people. He is also setting up viewing centres with standby generators all over the country where people can watch the concert. He is upbeat about it all.'

'Tell him I'm not going to do it!'

'I'm sure you will have the opportunity to tell him so yourself,' Mr Player replied in a frosty voice.

'Yes, I will tell him to his face.'

Mr Player turned and walked away.

The square was a very sad place that night, without music and without stars in the night sky.

TWENTY-SEVEN

Soldiers invaded the square the following night, just as Taduno and his friends were preparing to go to bed. A truckload of them came, and they kicked everybody's arse and whipped them with *koboko*. Everyone scampered away into the night, and only Taduno remained. He knew that they were there for him and saw no point trying to run.

They seized him roughly and plunged a syringe filled with sedative into his arm, according to the instructions of the President. But then a couple of over-zealous soldiers took it in turns to pierce him with another syringe and another and another and another. And he became dead with sleep, as dead as a dead mule.

They bundled him into their truck and drove him across the border into a neighbouring country where the President had a good friend, also a dictator. They took him to a hilltop hospital – a mental asylum – and they dumped him on his back on a clean white bed in a clean white room.

He wasn't aware of where or how far they had taken him

because he was in a sleep of a dead mule. He lay there on his back in that country with no name, a country where the only name that could be mentioned was that of the dictator who ruled it. Everything was named after the dictator, even the people were named after him. He was the grand leader, the owner of the country and its people, and it was to this country that they took Taduno.

*

It was rainy season in that country, so the rain pelted the zinc roof above him ceaselessly while he slept. The President could not come to see him; it was pointless. He needed him to be awake to be able to talk to him. So he waited anxiously for him to come out of sleep.

One of the soldiers came up with a clever idea, one that made much sense to the dictator. They brought Lela to the asylum, cleaned her up and dressed her like a nurse, and instructed her to look after him.

She sat like a ghost in an armchair next to his bed and watched over him while he slept. At night, she crept into bed beside him and slept with her eyes partly open.

The people she saw appeared a little strange to her. They were of much darker skin, of a different look, and they spoke English with a different accent.

*

Taduno slept for over thirty days, and all that time she sat by his side and fixed a constant gaze upon his face. The

221

waiting stretched her endurance. It stretched her imagination more. She never knew that one could be so dead to life for so long and yet be so alive.

She left his side only to use the bathroom or to go to the adjoining room where they served her food. One day as she ate breakfast, a maid told her, 'This place is a mental asylum. You and your boyfriend are in a private ward, that's why you don't see any other patients around.'

'But why's Taduno in a mental asylum?' she asked. 'What am I doing here?'

The maid offered no answer.

Lela finished eating and returned to his side. She felt so alone, even though she was sitting right next to him, even though she could hear the gentle rising and falling of his chest.

They came to feed him through his nose with tubes. She couldn't bear to watch, so she would always turn her face away until they had finished and were out of the room. She felt very sad to see him like this. She never spared a second to think about herself or about the dingy cell where they had previously kept her. Her thoughts were totally focused on him, and her passionate prayers solely for his benefit.

*

And then one morning, more than thirty days after he was drugged by the President's men, he opened his eyes very slightly and then shut them again. A heavy rain was pouring that morning. He remained very still in bed, on his back. He opened his eyes a second time and everything appeared to be covered with the haziness of a dream, a white dream that seemed to stretch endlessly before him. He closed his eyes, as if to grasp the reality of things, to ascertain the authenticity of life, but the haziness of a dream remained. He did not hear anything, not even the unceasing musicality that spread a faint chill as the rain pelted the roof above him. Realising that he was expending too much energy trying to focus, he allowed himself to drift back into sleep.

By his bedside, Lela sat up in the armchair. She had noticed the movement of his eyelids and her brow creased into anxious lines as she reached out and took his hand, gently, so as not to startle him. She wondered what he saw when he opened his eyes. Did he see her? Did he recognise her? She waited for him to show further signs of life.

*

The next time he opened his eyes the rain had stopped, but the faint chill continued to spread, even now that a soundless musicality prevailed upon the world. She did not intend to allow him to slip away a second time. So when he opened his eyes, she called out his name softly.

He did not hear her, and all he could see was the hazy white dream. That was all he could hear too, and he wondered how it was possible to hear a dream. He noted that the world about him was eerily quiet, the kind of quietness that follows a storm or a great loudness. He frowned as he tried to understand it all.

Lela sensed his struggle. She called his name again, reaching out to take his hand. He turned in the direction of her voice. Lela? He saw her sitting in a chair staring intently at him and he wondered how she got there and what she was doing there. Where was there?

The frown on his face deepened as he stared back at her. He tried to open his mouth, but it was as if his lips had been glued together. He made a more determined effort, and this time succeeded in mouthing her name, 'Lela . . . ?' A pause. 'Is it you?'

Before she could say anything in response, a handful of soldiers swarmed the room. They had been watching them all this while, waiting for him to wake up. They had delivered her to the hospital so that she would be the first person he saw when he came out of sleep. Having served her purpose, they bundled her away.

TWENTY-EIGHT

The President visited him the next day, by which time Taduno's recollection of things was complete. No one had spoken to him since they bundled Lela away. He just lay there on his back in the white bed, drifting in and out of sleep.

They came to feed him once, not through his nose this time. He sat up in bed, they planted the tray of food on his lap, and he ate very slowly. He did not know what he was eating, did not care actually. He wondered where they had taken Lela and what they were going to do to her. He could not understand why they kept him in a white room. A mixture of stale smells teased his nostrils.

Without warning, the President walked into the white room. He wore his enigmatic smile and he came towards him like a long-lost friend. He looked very smart in a dark T-shirt and blue jeans. Taduno had never seen him dressed in that fashion before. He sat up in bed.

'Good to see you again, my friend!' the President greeted effusively. 'You have slept for a long time!'

Taduno just stared blankly at the man.

The President pulled back the armchair by his bed and sat down. 'I am so sorry my men drugged you so much. That was not my instruction and they have been duly punished.'

'Where am I? Where is Lela?' he managed to ask.

'Don't worry, you are in a safe country not far from our own. Lela is safe too. So please don't worry about her, for now.'

He sighed with frustration. 'Where is this place?'

'You are in the private ward of a mental hospital.' The President smiled, as if giving him a piece of good news.

'A mental hospital?'

'Yes, a mental hospital.'

'What am I doing in a mental hospital? Why did you bring me here? Why did you bring Lela here?'

'As I said, you are in a private ward, much nicer than the public ward. I'm sure you know what the public ward of a mental hospital looks like.' He paused. 'Mr Player told me you reneged on your promise and decided to go and live at TBS with homeless men. If you insist on being stubborn, this is where I intend to keep you and Lela . . . in the public ward, I mean. And I will leave the two of you here for the rest of your miserable lives.' He hardened his smile to prove his point.

Taduno stared.

'Let me tell you, the nurses in the public ward used to be mental patients themselves. So if you remain stubborn, I will leave you and Lela in their care for the rest of your lives.'

'You are a sick man.'

'No, I'm not. You are the patient here.' There was steel in the President's voice. 'Now I must leave,' he said, rising up. 'Mr Player will come to see you shortly. You can leave with him when you are ready to honour our agreement.'

'Wait! Where is Lela?'

But the President had already walked out of the white room.

He shut his eyes and groaned, 'TK, you said a miracle will come. Where is that miracle now?' The anguish of his own voice engulfed him in that room.

*

He was surprised to see Mr Player looking so very frail when he walked in, as if he hadn't eaten in weeks, or as if he had been through severe torture. His hair looked unkempt and he hadn't shaved in a long time.

'What happened to you?' he asked with concern.

Mr Player sighed, a soft tired sigh. 'They kept me in the public ward all this while,' he said in a small voice.

'They brought you here too?'

'Yes, and they kept me in the public ward.'

'Oh my God.' Taduno raised a hand to his mouth.

'Let's make the music and end this whole ordeal, I beg you. If not for your sake, do it for Lela's sake, do it for my sake. This place is worse than hell . . .'

'Do you know where they took Lela?' he asked after a short silence.

'I don't know, I haven't seen her. Look, they could keep us here for the rest of our lives, and we could grow

227

to be ninety, even a hundred. Let's make the music, I beg you.'

Taduno bowed his head in thought for a long time. When he looked up, his eyes were two lifeless stones. 'You may leave my room now,' he said tersely.

'What?' Mr Player said in a startled voice.

'I said leave my room now!'

Mr Player clasped his hands on his head and began to cry. 'You got me into this whole mess in the first place. I was minding my own business when you came to me. Look at me now. Look at me!' He spread out his hands hopelessly.

Two soldiers came in to take Mr Player away.

Taduno broke down in tears when they had left.

*

He languished in that white room for two more days. On the third day, he sent for a soldier and told him he was ready to leave with Mr Player.

'Are you sure you are well now?' the soldier asked.

'Yes,' he replied.

'No more mental illness?'

'No more mental illness.' His voice was detached.

'For your own sake I hope you don't have a relapse by annoying Mr President again.'

He ignored the soldier's words. 'Tell Mr Player that we are ready to leave, please.'

The soldier shrugged. 'As you wish, sir.'

'And Lela too. I want her to come with me.'

The soldier laughed quietly. 'That's impossible, sir.'

'Why not?'

'Mr President took her with him.'

'Took her where?'

'I don't know,' he said, with a shrug. 'Even if she were here I do not have the authority to release her to you. Only Mr President can do that.'

'Can I see Mr President, please?'

'No, you cannot.'

'Why not?'

'Because he has left.'

He could not hide his irritation. 'Okay, go and get Mr Player, and get us out of here.'

*

They were driven across the border back to Lagos and taken straight to Mr Player's studio. Mr Player wanted them to start rehearsal immediately, but Taduno told him there was no need for that.

'Please don't tell me you are backing out again?' Mr Player's voice was desperate.

'No, I'm not backing out. I can't back out any more.'

Mr Player gave a huge sigh of relief. 'In that case let's start rehearsal straightaway. Mr President has put all the arrangements for the concert in place. We could record the song in three or four days' time, do the concert a day after, and then release the song after the concert. Mr President will be very happy with us.'

'There is no need for me to rehearse,' he responded quietly. 'I'm ready. You can do a live recording at the concert and release the song as you wish. That way, it will be original, straight from the heart.'

'We have to make sure we get it right,' Mr Player said uncertainly, 'or Mr President will be very displeased with us. And you know what that means.'

'Don't worry, I am ready whenever you are.' His voice betrayed no emotion, but there was something in it, and that something troubled Mr Player.

'Okay, I will double-check with Mr President to make sure everything is in place for us to go ahead.'

'Do that. By the way, I need you to go to TBS tomorrow and retrieve my guitar. Ask for Thaddeus, tell him I sent you.'

'We could just buy you a brand new one.'

'No, if I must play at this concert I must play with my old guitar.'

'Okay, I will get it tomorrow.'

'Thank you,' he said. He reached into his breast pocket and touched Lela's last letter.

*

He could not go back to his house. He could not go back to the square. So he just roamed the streets, with a new fedora he bought at a bus stop covering his face. He could not wait for the moment he would take to the stage. He knew it would be his last time. He knew that some would consider him a traitor, others a hero. To himself, he would always be a traitor. And that was why he must attempt to redeem himself with just one song. He would not have an opportunity for a second.

230

The city was abuzz about the forthcoming concert. And as Taduno roamed the streets he saw huge billboards of himself headlining the 'Great Concert'. He noticed that no reference was made to the President and he wondered why. In any case, he thought with a shrug, the whole country would be watching.

He suddenly felt hungry and he stopped at a roadside restaurant where he ordered *eba* and *egusi* soup. He ate with his fedora on so that no one could tell who he was. They saw him as a stranger, they admired his new fedora.

'I like your hat,' the woman who owned the restaurant said to him.

'Thank you.' His voice was quiet.

'Why do you eat with your hat covering your face?' she asked.

'Because I just bought it and I want to enjoy it as much as I can while I can,' he replied.

'It is a beautiful hat. I'd do the same if I were you,' she said with a smile.

He smiled back at her, but only with his lips; his eyes were hidden beneath the fedora and they were the eyes of a traitor.

He slept under a bridge that night, but he did not think of Lela. He had stopped thinking about her. His thoughts were only of the President.

*

The day of the Great Concert came, a Saturday, a day when everybody could watch. Feverish excitement gripped

231

the country. The national stadium was packed to over-flowing and so were all the viewing centres set up across the country.

When he stepped onto the stage there was a deafening ovation that seemed to last for ever. His eyes roamed the audience, and as he did so he saw the tall muscular assassin who carried a gun that fitted into his huge palm like a mere toy. He saw him in the front row in his black suit, black sunglasses and black shoes. He saw the blackness of his face which gave him the mien of a very angry man. He knew that the assassin was there to take him out in the event that he tried to deliver the wrong message, and he realised that his redemption song would be a very short one.

He held up his guitar for silence. And in a sad voice, he began to sing about a woman he dearly loved, a woman he was about to betray hopelessly.

He sang about love, about how love was doomed in the country they lived. 'I am a traitor,' he said, 'I have betrayed love, and I beg for forgiveness.' He told the people, 'I cannot betray you, so I must betray the one I love most, I must betray the one who taught me to love.'

He looked at his audience sadly, feeling like a hopeless traitor. And as they looked back at him, they somehow understood the sacrifice he was making for them. Some began to weep.

'Please don't cry,' he implored them with his guitar, 'dry your tears, my friend TK said a miracle will come.'

And then, addressing the President, he began to sing the last lines of his short song. 'So you see, where there is true love you can never win against love, you can never win against the people, we will not surrender to tyranny.' It was too late for Mr Player and the President to stop him. His face was sombre. He leaned back and allowed his guitar to echo his final words. His fingers danced franctically across the strings while his fans screamed in ecstasy.

It was far more time than he had hoped for. He saw the black assassin raise his gun. He reached into his breast pocket and touched Lela's letter one last time. He closed his eyes and begged love for forgiveness.

Acknowledgements

Victoria (BL), thank you so much for believing and for the solitary times you endured. A big thank-you too to Trevor Dolby, for showing me the way; Clare Christian, who rekindled my hope; my agent, Toby Mundy, who gave new life to this story; my wonderful editor, Louisa Joyner; Natasha Hodgson; Lorraine McCann; Alison Rae; 'The Big Man', Jamie Byng; and, of course, everyone at Canongate. My deepest gratitude goes to the Creator, who wrote this story through me.